The City and The House

Also by Natalia Ginzburg
and available in Seaver Books:

All Our Yesterdays
The Little Virtues
Family Sayings

The City and The House

Natalia Ginzburg

Translated from the Italian
by Dick Davis

SEAVER BOOKS
New York

First published in the United States in 1987 by Seaver Books,
333 Central Park West, New York, New York 10025.
Distributed by Henry Holt and Company, Inc.,
521 Fifth Avenue, New York, New York 10175.
Originally published in Italy under the title *La Città e la Casa*.

Library of Congress Cataloging-in-Publication Data
Ginzburg, Natalia.
The city and the house.
Translation of: La città e la casa.
I. Title.
PQ4817.I5C513 1987 853'.912 86–31563
ISBN: 0-8050-0392-4

First American Edition

Printed in the United States of America
1 3 5 7 9 10 8 6 4 2

ISBN 0-8050-0392-4

GIUSEPPE TO FERRUCCIO

Rome, 15th October

My dear Ferruccio,

I booked my ticket this morning. I leave in six weeks, on 30th November. I sent off my three trunks a week ago. There are books, suits and shirts in them. Phone me when they arrive. I know how much you prefer the telephone to letters. I'm the opposite.

I am very happy to be leaving. I am very happy that I'll see you again. My life here has become difficult recently. I couldn't breathe any more. When I decided to come and see you I was able to breathe again.

I am also very sorry to be leaving. I think I shall miss certain people and places I'm strongly attached to. I don't think I'll make new friends. I've become rather solitary over the years. I have had some friends here, not that many, and I shall miss them. But there has to be something to put up with. I shall be with you and that will mean a great deal to me. I am very fond of you, as you know, and I have been painfully aware of your absence all these years. Your visits were short, and few and far between. I enjoyed them, it's true, but at the same time they upset me because they were short and because I was always afraid I bored you; I was always afraid that being with me meant very little to you.

I often wonder whether you are pleased that I'm coming. True, it was you who told me to come, but sometimes I feel that perhaps you regretted this afterwards. But if you have had regrets, let's say no more about it at this stage. I have booked my ticket and I am definitely leaving. I will try to be as little financial trouble to you as I can.

I am coming to America like someone who has decided to

throw himself into the sea and hopes he will emerge either dead or new and changed. I know this kind of talk irritates you, but this is what I feel and I want you to know.

With love from,

Giuseppe

GIUSEPPE TO LUCREZIA

Rome, 20th October

My dear Lucrezia,

I don't think we shall see each other again. I think yesterday was the last time. I told you that I might come again, next Saturday, to Monte Fermo, but I don't think I shall. Yesterday evening as we were coming through the gate I looked up at *Le Margherite*, and I thought that I was looking at your house for the last time. I don't think I shall come and see you again. And I don't think you will come to Rome. There's no point. Don't come on my behalf. I said goodbye to you yesterday, and I don't like saying goodbye to people twice. Don't phone me, and I won't phone you either. I don't want to hear your voice, nor do I want you to hear mine. I prefer this sheet of paper.

You told me that you will come and see me in America. But I don't believe it. In all the years I've known you I've never seen you set off on a long journey. The only thing I've seen you do, in all these years, is to jump in your beat-up old Volkswagen that stinks of wet dog to get to the market in Pianura. And so I think the last time I'll see you was yesterday, on the station at Pianura. You had on your shaggy white woollen jacket with camels embroidered along the edge, and rather grubby white trousers, your hair was gathered on top of your head and one lock of it hung down on to your neck, and you were leaning against the wall. That's how I remember you. You were very pale. But then you are always pale. While he was waiting for the train to arrive, Piero said, 'Why don't you get the next one, it leaves in an hour?' I am very fond of Piero. I stood at the window and saw the three of you: you, Piero, Serena. Piero had his thick red scarf on. Serena was eating bread and cheese. You were leaning against the wall. That's how I remember you. Piero's sweetness and seriousness. His blond curls that are always a little greasy even when it's cold. Serena with her jumper covered in crumbs. Your height and pallor, the black lock of hair hanging down on to your neck, your hands in your pockets.

I shall do various things in the few days before I leave. At the moment I have to buy some shirts, a winter suit and an overcoat. Then I have to empty my flat. Not of its furniture but of everything which is of no use to anyone, old papers, old letters, old pots, old rags. Not the furniture, because as you know the Lanzaras are buying it with the furniture. Roberta says everything's going for a song. But you know how Roberta is. She immediately assigns every object a name, an importance and a financial value. I see Roberta a lot these days. She comes up and helps me empty the drawers. According to Roberta, my selling the house is a real piece of lunacy. Never sell bricks and mortar, never. You should hang on to bricks and mortar for dear life. And people have offered her immense sums for her flat, which is immediately under mine and is the same as mine, and she has refused them because she wouldn't dream of letting it go. But how is it possible that the Lanzaras are paying so little. My dear Giuseppe, she says to me, the Lanzaras are leading you up the garden path. And what will you do if one fine day you decide to come back? I answer that I don't think I'll ever want to do that. This is how we talk whilst we are emptying the drawers. Every so often we look at photographs of our relatives, and of when we were children, Ferruccio, Roberta and me, on the beach or skating.

The other day as we were walking in the woods Piero asked me 'Why are you going to America?' Usually when people ask me this I say the same things. I've no money. I'm tired of writing articles for newspapers. I'm sick of newspapers. My brother in Princeton knows a great many people. He teaches biology at the university and is very well thought of. He's lived there for many years. He'll find me a job. He has already made enquiries. I shall give Italian lessons in small schools. Teachers are well-paid in America. And then my brother is well-off and has no problems. I don't imagine I shall be completely dependent on him, but it's true that I will be to a certain extent. I shall do the housework and prepare meals. You know that I'm good at housework and very quick. I would like to live in Princeton, a tiny town that

I've never seen but which I can imagine because my brother has told me a lot about it. I would like to live in a tiny American town. I've never seen America and now I'll see it. I shall use the library at Princeton. There are lots of libraries there. I shall at last educate myself. I shall have peace in which to work and study and I don't ask for anything else. This is how I want to prepare myself for my old age. I have never managed to do anything and I am nearly fifty. I could go to America for a year and then come back. Well, I don't know. I don't like travelling. For some time now I've wanted to decide what to do, and then do it once and for all.

I like the idea of staying with my brother. He is only a little older than I am but he always led me and advised me when we were boys. I am an insecure person. I need someone who will reassure me. My brother is a man who has all the qualities I lack, he has a calm temperament and thinks clearly. I am very attached to my brother. But, said Piero, when your brother was here you were very depressed and seemed as if you hoped he would leave again. This is true. Having him in my house all the time wore me out. This is a house in which I am used to being alone. Finding him sitting in the living-room when I got up in the morning bothered me, and so did having to decide what he should do every day and who I should arrange for him to meet. Finding his striped dressing-gown in the bathroom bothered me. I'm not a hospitable person. I don't like having guests in the house, nor being the guest in someone else's house. But it won't be a question of guests in America: neither of us will be a guest. We shall be two brothers living together.

As soon as I get up in the morning I start to think of everything I am about to leave, of everything I am going to miss in America. I am leaving you. I am leaving your children, Piero, your house called *Le Margherite,* though goodness only knows why you called it that as no marguerites are to be seen there, nor even anywhere near. I am leaving the few friends I always saw at your house, Serena, Egisto, Albina, with whom we used to go for walks in the woods and with whom we used to play cards in the evening. I say 'used to' but this is a mistake, because you will continue to go for walks and to play cards, and the 'used to' refers only to me. I am leaving my cousin Roberta, a splendid, noisy, interfering, rough diamond of a woman who is devoted to everyone. I am leaving my flat here, where I have lived for more than twenty years. The fake-fur armchair with a plaid over it where I sit in the mornings as soon as I wake up. The four-poster bed with thin wooden columns where I finish up in the evenings. The kitchen window that looks on to the convent garden. The living-room windows that look on to via Nazario Sauro. The newspaper kiosk on the corner, the Mariuccia Restaurant that I occasionally go down to for a meal, the sports equipment shop and the Esperia Café. I am leaving you. I am leaving your broad, pale face, your green eyes, your black locks of hair, your swollen lips. We haven't made love now for three years, but when I see you I always have the feeling that we have done so yesterday. Whereas in fact we shall never do so again. That day at Viterbo you said 'Never again'. I am also leaving Viterbo behind, that hotel and that room I hated, and to which I returned by myself, last summer, for no reason whatsoever. Perhaps because I was very unhappy and I wanted to be even more so. I asked them to give me that exact room, number twenty-three. I often think about that room, and I shall think about it in America: I shall miss it, because we also miss places we have hated. But perhaps in America that room will be vaguer, more distant and innocuous. As for my son, I can't say I'm leaving him behind because I don't really know where he is, and I might see him more often in America, as long journeys are no problem for him.

Say goodbye to your children for me. I sort of said goodbye to them yesterday; I waved to them as I was passing through the kitchen where they were watching television and eating. I didn't want to stop and kiss them because I would have been upset and this would have been ridiculous to them; they would have carried away a ridiculous impression of me. Say goodbye especially to Cecilia, who is the child of yours I like best. You have told me that you think Graziano is my child, but you are probably mistaken, seen from behind he is just like your mother-in-law Annina. Cecilia has very beautiful eyes and she reminds me a little of my sister who died young. Daniele has a natural talent for drawing, as I did when I was a boy. Obviously neither Daniele or Cecilia are mine because they were born when I didn't know you, but what I mean is that I find something congenial in all your children except Graziano. Even the little one is quick-witted and charming. He isn't mine because he was born a year after Viterbo, and anyway he is identical to Piero. I find Graziano rather uninteresting, he's a real know-all. Perhaps it is those glasses that make him look like a little professor. The other four seem much nicer to me. But perhaps attributing the paternity of the least interesting of your children to me is part of your spitefulness against me.

Nevertheless, because you said Graziano is mine, I watched him carefully yesterday, whilst I was walking past and they were eating. He was eating a big plate of stew and polenta; he was serious, with his glasses on the end of that freckled nose of his. He was wearing his flannel pyjamas and was as red as a lobster, perhaps because he had just had a bath. That's how I remember him. None of your children are like you; they have freckles and red, puffy cheeks, none of them have your splendid pallor.

Anyway, believe me, none of your children is mine. They are all Piero's. He is an excellent father and they have no need of any other. The only child I have is Alberico. I would have liked someone different. But that certainly goes for him too. Who knows how many times he has thought that he would like to have a different father, someone other than me. When we are together we find it extremely difficult to say the simplest things to each other. I never say much about Alberico. I don't say much about him to anyone. I think my cousin Roberta has talked about him to you. I have a photograph of him hanging on the wall here, Roberta took it when he was five years old and my wife and I were still together. He was a beautiful child. I loved him, it's not difficult to love a child. I loved him but I never wanted to stay with him for very long. He soon bored me. I also have a photograph of my wife on the wall here, a frail girl enveloped in a shawl. She bored me too. All right, I was easily bored. I was very young and I was afraid of boredom. I am no longer so afraid of boredom but I was then. I was bored by my wife too. I found her stupid. I was bored with the child because he was a child, I was bored with her because she was stupid, and this was a particularly wearisome boredom. Before I married her I had not realized that she was so stupid, but then I gradually discovered how immensely stupid she was. She didn't find me stupid, though she did find me boring, and she found that I didn't give her enough of the things she wanted. Not enough love; not enough distractions and acquaintances; not enough money. And so Alberico spent the first years of his life with two people who were bored by each other. We separated. She and Alberico went to live in a flat in Trastevere. She took a lover, a cousin of hers who had been a childhood friend. She spent a lot of time away from the house and she left the child with Aunt Bice, a relation of my mother's. Two years after we separated she became ill during the summer and no one realized what was the matter with her. She had polio. We – Aunt Bice, her childhood friend and I – took her to a clinic. She was dead within a few weeks. Alberico was away at a summer camp and he had to be fetched. I didn't go; Aunt Bice went. Afterwards Aunt Bice always did everything. Alberico went to stay with her for good. My parents didn't want him because they said they were old and tired. My wife's parents were dead. I didn't want him because I just didn't feel up to it. The childhood friend had gone off to live in Venezuela. Alberico was taken to Aunt Bice's flat in via Torricelli, and he stayed there. Then Aunt Bice made her will and left everything she had to Alberico. And Aunt Bice was rich too. She didn't look it, but in fact she was rich. She was a general's widow.

Alberico was ten when he went to live in via Torricelli for good. He was a quiet, biddable, docile child and didn't cause any bother. He studied hard at school and he enjoyed it. Though I thought that all that boredom between my wife and me, which he had breathed in when he was little, must have poisoned him and that one day it would somehow or other burst out. I went to fetch him now and again and took him to the newspaper offices with me. At that time I had a steady job at the newspaper and I spent many hours every day there. Then I used to take him out to eat in a restaurant, and I'd take him to the cinema or to the Villa Borghese. I was bored and unsure of myself. I didn't know what to say to him. I talked about when I was a child. About my brother and me when we were children. About his mother. When I talked about his mother I tried to see her again as I had seen her when we first met, but this was not easy because memories of our later years immediately came to me. Alberico used to listen. He often mentioned Uncle Dé, his mother's cousin, the childhood friend. He seemed to me to be the person he cared most about in the world. When he mentioned him his face lit up. Uncle Dé had given him a stamp collection and a globe of the world. He occasionally sent him stamps from Venezuela. I used to take him home again and leave him at the front door, and go back to the newspaper with light, quick steps and a feeling of relief that I was alone again.

One day Alberico ran away from home. We found him a long way away two days later, at the end of Corso Francia. I remember that Uncle Dé, the childhood friend, had lived in that area while he was in Rome. Once or twice I thought to myself that I would write to Uncle Dé and suggest that he be in touch with Alberico as often as he could. But I didn't do it. I knew that Uncle Dé was working in a construction company in Venezuela, and that he was married. I think he soon stopped sending stamps.

Alberico ran away from home many other times, and we had to scour the city for him. Aunt Bice used to call me up and we spent days looking for him, in streets, in the public gardens, in police stations and railway stations. We would come across him sitting calmly in police stations, silent, in his blue anorak, with his little cardboard suitcase on his knees. He was very attached to that little suitcase and when he ran away from home he always took it with him. He kept cards of football players in it. When he was fourteen he still seemed to be a little boy. He had a rosy-pink complexion, with smooth cheeks and angelic curls. Now his curls are those of an old sheep, long, straggling, loose and soft; he always seems tired, and he has a short bristly beard; he is often dressed in black and looks like a hearse. When he laughs you see his marvellously white teeth. But then he doesn't laugh very often. I think all that boredom which he took in from his mother and me when he was little has now come to the surface, as I had expected it to. He started to read Political Science, then he left university and took up photography. But perhaps he would rather be a director – of films, or in the theatre – or an actor. He doesn't know. He's always changing his mind. It's very tiring for me to keep asking him what he wants to do. Actually I have never really known what I wanted to do either and I have spent my life asking myself. If I asked myself this without getting a clear answer, why should I expect a clear answer from him? At first I didn't mind working at the newspaper, then I became thoroughly disgusted with newspapers and now I'm leaving Italy. The difference between him and me is that I have no money, whereas at the moment he has, thanks to Aunt

Bice. On the other hand he is already twenty-five. He is a man. According to Roberta I ought to suggest something to him, but I don't know what kind of suggestion I could make. When I see him in front of me, my only concern is to annoy him as little as possible. Bore him as little as possible. I always think of that immense boredom that existed between me and his mother, which he drank in sip after sip, day after day, when he was a child.

The last time Alberico turned up was last April. He came from Agropoli. He was travelling with someone called Adelmo, a short, muscular, bandy-legged character. They left two identical rucksacks, stuffed to bursting, in the entrance hall downstairs, then they had a shower and flooded the bathroom which they left strewn with sweatshirts, vests and socks. I called Roberta up, because Roberta feels very sympathetic towards Alberico and makes it easier for me to be with him. I left them in the front room and washed the sweatshirts, vests and socks. Then I made *trenette col pesto*. Whilst we were eating Alberico said that he wanted to sell the flat in via Torricelli, the one that Aunt Bice had left him. Roberta was alarmed. Never sell bricks and mortar, never. You have to hang on to bricks and mortar for dear life. Alberico said that he wanted to move to the country and raise rabbits and chickens. He and Adelmo went off to bed. I had made a bed up in the room at the end of the corridor, the one I call 'Alberico's room' even though he has hardly ever slept there. Roberta and I were left alone together. She asked me if I knew that Alberico often went to the California Bar. I told her that I didn't know anything, and that I didn't even know where the California Bar was. She said it was in the via Flaminia area and that it was a foul place. I didn't sleep a wink that night. In the morning I sat in the front room making up questions and phrases and repeating them to myself under my breath. But when I saw Alberico in front of me all those questions and phrases stuck in my throat. He and Adelmo were already dressed and ready to leave. I made them coffee and toast. Whilst they were eating they talked quietly about their own affairs. The vests and socks I had washed for them were still wet but they wrapped them in towels and newspapers and stuffed them into their rucksacks anyway. They were off to London they told me. But two weeks later I heard that they had been arrested in the California Bar. The whole California Bar finished up in prison. Alberico was in prison for a month, you know this because I've told you about it. I was waiting for him at the prison gate when he came out. Roberta told me he was coming out, she had heard it from the lawyer we had engaged. I watched him emerge, he was listless and tired, calm, in a thick leather coat with a bundle of clothes under his arm. Adelmo wasn't with him. Instead he had with him a plump, red-haired character dressed in grass-green overalls. I asked him where Adelmo was but he said he didn't know anything about him. I asked him to come back home with me; he said he might come for lunch but at the moment he had things to do. He offered me his hand and I kissed his thin, black, bristly beard. Then I saw them disappear side by side – the green overalls and the leather coat – along the Lungotevere. He didn't come to lunch that day and for a while I heard nothing about him. Then I heard that he had sold the flat in via Torricelli. Roberta told me. He had got a good price for it. He's sly, Roberta said to me, he doesn't look it but he's sly; he loves money and always knows how and where to get hold of it. What makes you think he loves money I asked her, this love of money isn't apparent in the way he lives. You don't know him, Roberta said. It's certainly true that I don't know him. A few days ago he wrote to me from Berlin. He's working on a film. For the moment he doesn't intend to come back to Italy. Perhaps after the winter. The letter had the address of an hotel on it. I phoned him and told him that I was going to live in America. He said it seemed a good idea. I asked him to come and say goodbye to me before I left. He told me that he didn't think he could travel, because of the film. We would see each other in America, in some American city where one day or other he might happen to turn up. The film is a film about Ulysses. He is the assistant director but they have also given him a little part, the part of a shepherd who sits on a rock and plays a pipe.

I shall go to the cemetery before I leave. I haven't been there for quite a while. My parents are there, and Aunt Bice, and in another part away from them, my wife. Aunt Bice is the one I think of most often. She was stupid and full of good will and above all full of an immense faith in herself. This faith filled the rooms, the sideboards and the balconies of her house. She was an optimist and was quite certain that everything she came across, every thing she could see and touch, would turn out well and happily. No one wanted Alberico; she didn't have a moment's hesitation, she immediately took him in. She had sky-blue eyes that were clear as water, a great head of white hair and a radiant smile. When we went wandering through the streets looking for Alberico and we couldn't find him that smile faltered a little, but only a little. When she died Alberico was nineteen. He was doing his military service in Messina. I don't know if Aunt Bice had ever realized that Alberico was a homosexual. I don't think so. There were no homosexuals in her world. She died more or less unexpectedly, of a heart-attack, while visiting a neighbour. But she must have felt ill a few days before because she had contacted her solicitor. Then she had written a letter to Alberico but she hadn't had time to post it, it was in her handbag. She had drawn up a list of every thing she had and left it to him – the flat in via Torricelli, her stocks and shares, three shops in Naples and some gold in a safe deposit. Lastly she asked him to look after her cat. Alberico came for the funeral and immediately went off again. The cat was entrusted to a neighbour. When he had finished his military service Alberico came to fetch it and took it to a flat where he was staying with some friends. He didn't come and live in via Torricelli for the moment. He preferred his friends' flat, a commune where six of them were living. He took the cat in a dome-shaped basket that he had bought specially. But as soon as the cat arrived in the commune it escaped over the roofs and was lost.

Later Alberico went to live in via Torricelli with one of his friends, a Brazilian painter called Enrique. There were photographs everywhere, hanging from strings to dry, and Enrique's paintings of forests and jaguars were everywhere too. Aunt Bice's flat became a den in a few days. Now the den has been sold and there is no trace anywhere of Aunt Bice's optimism or of her faith in herself, or of her blue polka-dot aprons and white fat legs and spongy down-at-heel slippers.

Egisto has just phoned me. He will call here and we shall have dinner together somewhere. I shall give this letter to him and he can take it to you on Saturday, because as I have already told you I shall not be coming on Saturday.

Giuseppe

EGISTO TO LUCREZIA

Rome, 25th October

I meant to come to *Le Margherite* today but I shan't because the spark-plugs on my Dauphine are dirty, and anyway I have to finish an article. I tried to phone you but there was no answer. That Sicilian you have now must be deaf. The one you had before, from the Abruzzi, was better.

I have a letter for you from Giuseppe and I will give it to Albina who is coming by train. I will also give her these few lines of mine.

I'm sorry, I would have liked to have come to stay with you and play tennis with Piero. It's true that your tennis-court is wretched after that last storm, it's full of holes and the last time I almost sprained my ankle. But it doesn't matter.

I met a very pleasant person the other night, at the Rotunnos'. He is called Ignazio Fegiz and he is a picture-restorer. He took me home because I had come on foot. He has an olive-green Renault. He is very intelligent. If you like, when I come next Saturday I will bring him with me. You have that still-life Piero bought in Salerno, the one that is full of stains and cracks, and perhaps you could have him look at it. It seems a mess to me but I know that Piero values it. He will be able to tell you how to get rid of the stains, and perhaps even the cracks too.

I've seen Giuseppe. He seems to me very depressed. We were supposed to go and eat in a restaurant but then his cousin arrived and asked if we would like to eat something downstairs with her. She is called Roberta. I think you know her, she has come to *Le Margherite* a few times. She is blonde, with big hips, and big teeth that stick out. She is a cheerful, interfering, busybody of a woman. We went down and she made us spaghetti in a very complicated way that I can't remember. It involved spinach, cream and eggs. The spinach was frozen, that I know. She is on a diet and didn't eat the spaghetti. She only ate an apple and a little plate of chicory without oil or salt.

Roberta's flat is similar to Giuseppe's but bigger. She and I talked about flats. Giuseppe has sold his. I think he has made a real cock-up of it. He had already been to the solicitor's and signed the contract. A family called Lanzara are buying it. He is a psychoanalyst who is quite well-known.

With the money from the sale of that flat Giuseppe is going to buy some Treasury Bonds. So he will have something if he decides to come back. Or they will be there for his son if he should need them. His son is rich because he inherited a lot from an aunt, but he has no desire to do anything. He has been in prison on a drugs charge. He's a lost soul.

Princeton is a tiny, very beautiful town. It was founded by the Quakers. It has big parks and lots of trees. The trees are full of squirrels. When Giuseppe opens his windows he will see squirrels. But I think he will soon come back here, in less than a month. America is not at all his kind of place. It's because he no longer wants to go that he is so depressed.

We'll see one another next Saturday, I'll bring Ignazio Fegiz.

Egisto

LUCREZIA TO GIUSEPPE

Monte Fermo, 26th October

Albina gave me your letter and also one from Egisto. She rummaged in her handbag with that greenish lizard's claw of hers and pulled out first a handkerchief, then a comb, and then some tampax and then the two letters. I was in the kitchen bottling wine with my mother-in-law and that general help who arrived a few days ago from Piazza Armerina and who has no idea how to help do anything at all.

I left them all there and came up to my room and locked myself in.

What a strange person you are. We've said almost nothing to each other for so long and then all of a sudden you write me a long letter. There was a period when we wrote each other letters, you and I, but there weren't many of them and they weren't very long either, and that period was quite some time ago, four, five years ago. Afterwards we didn't write to each other any more and neither did we talk to each other very much. How many times have we been alone together during these years, you and I, how many times have we gone for long walks in the woods, and you said nothing more than 'How are things?' and 'What are you doing?', and I was just the same.

I don't know why you say I'm spiteful to you. It's not true. I don't have any spiteful feelings for you. I wouldn't have any reason to. We had an affair which lasted a few years and ended. A simple story.

You annoy me when you say that Graziano is an insignificant child. It's not true. None of my children is insignificant. All five of them are very special and very good-looking. Everyone says so.

Graziano is yours. But if you prefer to pretend that he isn't, it doesn't matter.

In your letter you mention only four of the children. You don't mention Augusto. I don't know why. Perhaps he is the one that is most like me. Even if he has red cheeks and not 'my splendid pallor'.

I was pleased that you wrote that phrase. It re-echoed in my head all day long. Every so often I go in front of the mirror to look at 'my splendid pallor'.

Today I am going to Pianura with Serena and Albina. Serena has got it into her head to open a 'centre'. Her landlord's family have a warehouse. Serena has asked them if she can rent it. Serena is bored. She wants to open a centre in this warehouse which she will call 'The Women's Centre'. There will be a library and meetings once a week on Friday evenings. We shall recite poetry and act plays together. Serena enjoys acting. She particularly enjoys acting Alfieri's *Mirra*. Serena was a very bad student and she can't remember anything of what she studied, but she does remember Alfieri's *Mirra,* goodness only knows why. She wants to be able to stand in a theatre, in front of people who have come to listen, and say, 'When I asked you/ You should have given me the sword, Euriclea/ I would have died innocent/ Now I shall die guilty.' *Mirra* is the story of someone who is in love with her father. Though Serena has never been in love with her father. No, not even in her wildest dreams. But she says that when she thinks of that ending it always makes her want to cry.

What a strange person you are. In your letter you tell me about your son. You have never talked about him to me, nor to Piero, nor I think to the others. When we asked you about him you always answered briefly and changed the subject. But I know everything about your son, from Roberta. I already knew what you wrote to me. Aunt Bice, the cat, the California Bar.

Later.

I don't know why you think I feel spiteful towards you. No, not at all. Why should I. We had an affair that lasted for quite a while. Then it finished. Simple.

I wanted to leave Piero and come and live with you. It would have been a big mistake, but I didn't see this. It would have been a mistake because we were already tired of each other, you of me and I of you. But I didn't see it, I hadn't realized. You told me that I should not leave Piero, that I shouldn't even think of doing so. You said the children would suffer. I said that I would bring them with me and they wouldn't suffer much; Piero could have seen them sufficiently often. That house where you live is big enough and with a few little rearrangements we could have all fitted in. Then you got very frightened. I read the fear on your face. You probably envisioned your house being turned into a camp-site. I don't know how to tell you how much that fear of yours hurt me. You said that you didn't feel up to being a father to the children. You didn't feel you could take on the role of father. Your usual obsession. You are always afraid that someone will make you take on the role of a father. Then I told you that you were a coward. We were in your house. You hate that hotel in Viterbo, but I hate your house. I decided that day not to go back there ever again. But as it turned out I went back there a couple of times, later on.

That day I broke some ashtrays too, not just one but three or four. I grabbed the ashtrays I saw within reach and hurled them on the floor. You knelt down on the carpet to pick up the pieces and I cried. I despised you and I cried.

I don't remember the name of that hotel in Viterbo. I remember there were red curtains that had a vile smell. We talked very calmly, sitting on the bed. Then we went out and went to the cinema. *The Four Feathers* was on. I can't remember anything about the film. Just the name. I cried, my tears cascaded down, but you took no notice.

After Viterbo I fell in love two or three times. Once with one of Piero's clients, someone who had a ceramics shop in Perugia. But he was always worrying about his financial affairs and took no notice of me. Another time with an English archaeologist, a friend of Serena's. Neither time was it very important and it was quickly over. As you know I fall in love easily. Months passed, I was sad and I thought I wanted another child, because I like being pregnant. At first Piero was rather against this, and then he accepted it. When Vito was three months old I stopped feeding him with my milk and I couldn't find the right way to wean him. I was recommended to a doctor. He came from Perugia almost every day to see Vito and sometimes he stayed for lunch. I waited for him very anxiously because he used to reassure me, and perhaps waiting so anxiously made me fall in love with him. I think you saw him at our house once, his name was Civetta.

He was neither handsome nor young, he was white-haired and he stooped a little. I went to bed with him twice, in his surgery in Perugia. But it wasn't anything important and I didn't mention it to Piero. Only Serena knew. But he told his wife, he had a short, plump wife who was always walking around Perugia with a little dog. His wife said he shouldn't see me again. He immediately agreed. Then he was transferred to Vicenza. All the same, for a while I continued to wear his tattered old red and black check jersey, which he had left on a peg in the hall and forgotten, and then never asked for it back, and Piero used to ask me how ever I could wear that horrible jersey that reminded him of Doctor Civetta and that time when I couldn't find the right way to wean Vito.

One day when I was crying Piero asked me if I was crying because of you. There were two or three Saturdays when you didn't come and you had phoned to say you couldn't because you were writing something or other. But that time I wasn't crying because of you, I was just crying, for no earthly reason. Then Piero said that you had many fine qualities but that you lacked back-bone. He kept consoling me as though I were crying for you, even though I kept telling him that everything with you had been over for a long time.

Today I was at the Women's Centre with Albina and Serena and we cleaned up the floor a bit, then Serena climbed up a ladder because there are two little windows with grimy glass covered in cobwebs. She wiped them with newspapers while I held the bucket for her, but they stayed grimy from top to bottom just as before.

Albina and Serena say that I should come to Rome and talk to you and persuade you to stay in America for a fortnight or a month but no longer. They say America is not your kind of place. But I think you will enjoy being in America and if I had a brother in America who said to me come and stay here for good, I would go immediately. I would take all my children and go. But I don't have any brothers, neither in America nor anywhere else, and you are lucky that you have this brother in Princeton, a town that's full of squirrels and trees. A town that must be solid, orderly, clean and hospitable. You will say that here I have all the trees I could want and that though there aren't any squirrels, there are lots of other animals, cats and dogs and rabbits and hens. Our place is smothered in trees and animals. Since I was a girl I've wanted to live in the country and have lots of children. I have had what I wanted, but meanwhile I've become a different person. The children are fine, but I've had it up to here with the country. I want to have a town around me: Princeton. Instead, I only have fields and woods around me. If I stand at the window and look at this countryside with its fields and woods and vines I don't feel a sense of peace but of fear. When we bought this house I thought it was really beautiful – so big and yellow and old, but now there are days when I can't bear it, not the front nor the back nor inside it. If I make the effort to get to Monte Fermo, I find a village of fifteen houses leaning over a ravine, of old women sitting on steps, and of hens. If I make the effort to get to Pianura I don't find a town but another village, a big crowded noisy unpleasant village and I'm fed up to the back teeth with that too.

I told Piero that we could sell this house and go and live in Perugia or even in Rome. He doesn't want to hear of such a thing. He is happy here. He doesn't see the countryside much because he spends his days in Perugia and only comes back here in the evenings. He is only here on Saturdays and Sundays and friends come then and he likes it.

Later still.

As far as your son is concerned, I want to say that if he won't come and say goodbye to you before you go, you should go and say goodbye to him. But you don't even think of such a thing. You just break things off with hardly a word. You let him go with hardly a word. You should at least feel a little curiosity, find out whether he is getting on all right in Berlin and how this film of his is going. What do you mean he is already twenty-five. Someone can suffer from the absence of his parents at twenty-five, even if it is he who wants to be away from them because he has decided that he doesn't like them at all. But he will be secretly pleased if his parents run after him.

At twenty-five I had been married for three years and I already had two children, nevertheless my mother still gave the orders and I obeyed them. I phoned her ten times a day to ask her how I should dress and what I should cook and she answered everything point by point in that thick voice of hers. I had married Piero because she liked him, she thought him a good man, serious, calm, 'a worker'. I married Piero because he was 'a worker'. She made me see everything she liked through rose-tinted spectacles. She even liked Signora Annina, Piero's mother, who is in fact a pest, and she and Signora Annina went off on little trips together. When I married Piero I realized that I had done well, reasonably well, but I knew that in marrying him I had only obeyed my mother. Then we lived in Florence, my mother in one house and Piero and I in another, in the same street. Signora Annina was living in Lucca and appeared every now and then. My mother had chosen our house, she had even chosen the furniture and the disposition of the rooms. My mother was a strong, robust, energetic woman who went about the city every morning busying herself with prisoners' families. She went marching around the city with her military step and flat shoes and a bag over her shoulder. She had a thick, deep, hoarse voice. After I got married she lived alone, with a serving woman called la Lina, and in the evenings she and la Lina knitted things, always for prisoners' families. With my mother, Piero and la Lina I felt protected, safe, secure; it seemed to me that they would keep every danger, every disaster away from me. Then my mother became neurotically depressed. But you know that, I've already told you. She began to complain of headaches and insomnia. The doctor examined her but there was nothing wrong, she was healthy. Bit by bit she stopped going out of the house, washing herself, eating and knitting. She sat in an armchair in her drawing-room, in semi-darkness, with her hands in her lap, and stared at a point on the carpet. When I phoned it was always la Lina who answered, by that time my mother didn't move, and when I went to see her she gave me a faint smile with half her mouth, then she immediately lowered her eyes and stared at the carpet. In a short time she became very old and thin, a shrunken frame with clothes hanging loosely on it. To me it seemed as if the world had been turned upside down. The doctor came all the time, he would sit down next to her and ask her questions which she hardly answered in her voice that was still hoarse and thick but also now harsh and grating. The doctor was young but not particularly good-looking, he was just very kind and I fell in love with him, because I always fall in love with doctors, but it wasn't anything important, he didn't realize and it soon passed. My mother was committed to a hospital for nervous disorders. La

Lina went back to her village in Sardinia. Piero got a job in Pisa in a refrigerator factory, a job which seemed to be much better than the one he had had in Florence, and so I had to empty my house and my mother's too. Piero was busy with his new job, and he also had problems with one of his superiors whom he didn't like, he was tired and in a bad mood and he told me to get on with it all by myself because he didn't have time and besides I was twenty-five years old. And so I no longer had any protectors. My mother stayed in that hospital for three months. I went to be with her as much as I could and I waited for her to say a few words to me; but she didn't say anything to me, she just gave me that faint smile with half her mouth every so often. One night she died, of a heart seizure. Piero had a furious row with his superior and was fired. We had only just settled in the new house in Pisa. Signora Annina, my mother-in-law, came to lend us a hand, but she did nothing except complain about the heat, the mosquitoes and the house. And we had very little money. Piero sat all day in our bedroom, smoking and staring at the window, and I looked at his big head with its blond curls that had become dark with sweat, and I would ask him what we should do now and he would raise his eyebrows and turn the corners of his mouth down. Certainly, I had no protectors any more. Then, that summer, I met Serena. Meeting her cheered me up. She was looking after children as an *au pair* with a Dutch family. When the Dutch family left she came to our house to look after our children. We became friends. She was no protection, on the contrary it was we who had to protect her, and comfort her when she cried. Serena often cries. She was hopeless with the children because she had no patience. In fact I stopped paying her almost at once. Anyway, she didn't need money because her father was rich and he looked after her. Serena phoned her father and asked him to find a job for Piero. Her father found him one. And that's how we left for Perugia, at the end of that summer. Piero immediately cheered up when he had a job. It has always been his dream to work in a legal office and he liked Doctor Corsi, his boss, a lot. He liked Perugia, he liked the office, he liked everything. Serena came to Perugia with us. Later on, when we bought *Le Margherite,* she took that room over the cinema in Pianura.

I haven't told you much new. You know many things about

me, I 've told you them a thousand times. But it was to tell you how I was and what happened to me when I was twenty-five.

I will say goodbye after this extremely long letter, and go and prepare supper because if I wait for the Sicilian to do it I'll be in a real mess.

Egisto has written to me saying he wants to come here on Saturday with someone he likes, but I don't want to see people at the moment. I feel depressed. Perhaps I'm sorry that you are going. I won't say don't go, or go only for a few days, but when you are there I shall miss you from time to time.

Lucrezia

LUCREZIA TO EGISTO

Monte Fermo, 27th October

Just a couple of lines to tell you not to bring the picture-restorer, or at least not to bring him this Saturday, because I'm worn out and I don't want to see him. I don't want to find myself face to face with someone I don't know. Piero doesn't want anyone to touch the still-life. One of his clients at the office told him it was enough to gently rub an onion over it a few times and the stains would disappear and the colours come up fresh again. He has been doing this for a few days and he is satisfied with the results.

Lucrezia

ALBINA TO GIUSEPPE

Rome, 28th October

Yesterday evening I phoned you when I got back from Monte Fermo, but you were out. I wanted you to ask me over for supper because my fridge was empty. So I phoned Egisto, he was in and came over straightaway; he had some more or less stale bread in his house and a tin of Campbell's soup, and we made ourselves a little soup.

I had two letters from Lucrezia, one for you and one for Egisto. I'll put yours in your post box when I pass your house on the way to school, and I'll add this note of mine, just a few words.

Egisto and I, and all of us, think you are making a mistake in moving to America for good. We think you will be very unhappy there. Go there for a holiday and come back. It doesn't matter if you have sold your flat, it doesn't matter if you have sent off your trunks, because there's a solution for everything.

It seems terrible that you're leaving Italy for good. It will be boring at *Le Margherite* without you. I shall certainly go there anyway, because I never have anything to do on Saturday and Sunday; if I go to see my family at Luco dei Marsi I'm ill for the whole week and if I stay in Rome I get depressed. So I shall go there anyway, but it won't be the same without you.

When I met you I fell in love with you, and now I want to tell you so. And I wrote you a lot of letters, but I tore them up. Then it was all over because I'm like Lucrezia in that way, I fall in love easily and then one day I wake up and it's all over.

I've never fallen in love with Egisto perhaps because he seems rather ugly to me – so squat and short and dumpy. Not that you are so good-looking to tell the truth, because you are dry and thin and sallow. Once or twice Egisto has asked me to go to bed with him, I said no, and he was hurt, because he's very touchy;

he disappeared for a few days then he came back again and everything was as before. Now we love each other like brother and sister. If I happen to go to bed with someone I tell him about it, but that doesn't happen often, because I fall in love easily but bed is a problem for me.

I don't get on with my real brother. I don't even get on with my mother and when I go home to Luco dei Marsi I have a terrible time. My father is the best, though he is old and deaf. Then there are my sisters Maura and Gina, one nine and the other ten. My brother works in a greengrocer's. He studied to be a teacher but couldn't find a job. It infuriates him that I have a job in Rome. He won't leave it alone. When I go in the shop where he works he gets sulky and goes off in a corner. Then he tells my mother that everyone thinks there is something peculiar about me and that they ask if perhaps I haven't finished up in the Red Brigade.

My mother and brother say I go around dressed like a beggar. I answer that I have to send a good proportion of my salary to them. They answer that I could go to a Standa department store and that I needn't spend much. They really hate my jeans and cheap shoes.

And then at home I have to sleep with Maura and Gina. It's really awful sleeping with Maura and Gina. All of us sleep in a big double bed with a red quilt. I'm too hot, they're too cold, I push the quilt off, they haul it back again. They chatter away in the dark to each other nineteen to the dozen, they giggle and shriek with laughter. When I got the job in Rome and found my bedsit, I was particularly happy in the evenings when I got into my little bed by myself. I've no idea why people say being alone is so unpleasant. Being alone in Rome is lovely. It's not so nice on Sundays if you are waiting for the phone to ring and it doesn't. On the other days it's lovely.

I would be very happy to make a little trip to America too, but I don't even have enough money to buy myself a new pair of shoes.

You must have heard about the Women's Centre. Yesterday we spent hours cleaning the floor. We were ready to drop afterwards. We went back to *Le Margherite* and Lucrezia shut herself in her room to write to you and told me to give Vito his supper. This was quite a job because Vito runs from one room to another and you have to follow him with the plate. Yesterday that Swiss girl they were expecting arrived. But she had taken the dogs for a walk. She says she adores dogs. Perhaps she prefers the dogs to the children, and she's quite right to because though Lucrezia's children are very beautiful they're quite impossible to put up with.

Afterwards Piero took me into Pianura by car, just in time for me to catch the last train.

I wanted to write you just a couple of words, and instead I have written you a proper, long letter.

Ask me over to supper tonight. Ask Egisto over too. You have to spend a little money on these suppers you keep giving us, but these are the last days you will be with us.

Albina

EGISTO TO LUCREZIA

Rome, 30th October

Disagreeable. You really are disagreeable. You don't want me to bring Ignazio Fegiz to see you, and I won't bring him. So much the worse for you. You will miss the opportunity of meeting a really agreeable person.

I'm sending you this letter by post. I'm not coming either. I'm going to Tarquinia with Ignazio Fegiz, to stay with some of his friends who have a beautiful house there.

Look after your still-lives and your onions.

Egisto

EGISTO TO LUCREZIA

Rome, 4th November

I apologise. My letter was a bit curt. Piero phoned me and apologised. He said that these days you are depressed and irritable. Perhaps Giuseppe's leaving has made you depressed. It's made all of us depressed. I apologised too. Piero said I was to bring whoever I liked.

I will come with Ignazio Fegiz next Saturday. We didn't go to Tarquinia because his friends asked us to postpone the trip, their water system had broken down.

Egisto

GIUSEPPE TO LUCREZIA

Rome, 5th November

The Lanzaras came today. I told you, they are the people who are buying my house. They came to look at the house and furniture properly and to decide on how the rooms should be arranged. I called Roberta and she came up immediately. I wanted her to meet them, seeing that she says they have led me up the garden path. Also Roberta has a way of making me more at ease with people. She had some caviar and brought it along. I made tea and toasted some bread. I like the Lanzaras. He is a psychoanalyst. He is little and has a long pear-shaped head which is completely bald. She is a plump Spaniard with black hair. They don't look like a couple of crooks. I would be very sorry if my home were to be lived in by a couple of crooks.

Whilst we were having tea Egisto arrived with a friend of his whom he has talked about a lot to me. He is called Ignazio Fegiz. When he came in, in a raincoat covered in epaulettes and buttons and with a peaked cap on his head, it seemed as if a great gust of wind came in with him. He is a man of about forty, but his hair is completely grey as was apparent when he took off his cap. A thick grey crew-cut. He is tall, good-looking, florid, with strong white teeth. He always keeps one hand clenched behind his back, and he makes great gestures in the air with the other. He sat down and had tea and ate a considerable amount of toast and caviar. He was meeting the Lanzaras for the first time but he immediately started to question them about the flat and the arrangement of the rooms, disapproving of everything they had already decided. He began to wander about the flat, flinging all the doors open. He discovered that they had to get rid of a wall between the kitchen and the bathroom, and make a new bathroom where the little cards-room is. They ought to have what is now the sitting-room as the bedroom and the room at the end of the passage should be the consulting-room. Roberta didn't agree. He got hold of a piece of paper and drew a plan of the flat as he saw it. Roberta drew a plan too. The Lanzaras stayed silent and seemed a little mystified. Egisto was curled up in a corner reading a book.

Then the Lanzaras left and I suggested that we make a little supper. Roberta started to make a sauce for the spaghetti. But Ignazio Fegiz also had his own ideas about spaghetti sauce. It didn't need butter and tomatoes, it needed oil, garlic and chillies. Egisto sided with him. I was neutral. Ignazio Fegiz won. I think he is one of those people who always wins.

While we were eating Ignazio Fegiz talked about himself. He lives alone. He has a flat in via della Scrofa. He restores pictures and sometimes he sells pictures too. When he was young he would have liked to paint, but he soon realized that he did not have a vocation for it.

He gives the impression of being an extrovert, expansive person who is generous with himself. But in fact I think he is a complicated, tormented person and that he has a whole lot of things inside himself that he never mentions. In that hand which he always keeps behind his back he has a bundle of things that he never shows to anyone. I said as much to him. I said that I would like to see what he had in that bundle. He burst out laughing and spread his hands out on the table. He laughed, but perhaps he wasn't too pleased all the same.

I feel I would like to stay here a little longer. But it is better that I leave thinking that my life here in Italy was a good one. In fact it seems good to me because I am leaving. Before I decided to leave I found it intolerable.

I would like to come to Monte Fermo once more. To go walking with you, to follow you through the streets in Pianura while you bought ham and wool. But I won't do it. I won't come. It's strange how sometimes a man forbids himself to do things he really wants to do, things that are completely harmless and simple and natural. But I shan't come. My separation from you has already happened. I'm already a long way off, already in America. I prefer sheets of paper.

I wander around Rome a great deal. Yesterday I took the bus to Piazza San Silvestro. Piazza San Silvestro isn't so very special, with its half-open bags of rubbish in the corner, its Japanese tourists, its beggars stretched out on newspapers, its post office vans and Red-Cross sirens and police motor-cycles. It isn't very special. But I said goodbye to it lovingly and for a long time. In America there will be other squares with tourists, beggars and sirens. But they will mean nothing to me because a man can only make so many things his own during his life. At a certain point in our lives everything we see for the first time is external to us. We look at it like tourists, with interest but coldly. It belongs to other people.

You say a lot about your mother in your letter. You have often talked about her to me. You never talk about your father because you can't remember him, he died when you were little. But I think that all your life you have been searching for a father, in your mother, in your husband, and in me. Perhaps you were even looking for a father in Dr Civetta.

I always say very little about my parents. I soon stopped thinking of them as any protection. I found them irritating and boring. I too drank in boredom as a child, it's true not as much as my own son, but I drank in my share. It was my brother who was a protection for me. Even now I feel the need for his authoritative, slightly contemptuous and high-handed protection. You often reproached me for not protecting you. But how could I have protected you when I myself have such a need to be protected? And you reproached Piero too for not protecting you. You often talk about your wish to feel protected. You often talk about protectors. It is one of your obsessions. 'Prostitutes have protectors,' Piero said to you once. You were very hurt. In truth, adults should not need to be protected. But perhaps neither you nor I have ever become adults, nor Piero either. We are a brood of children.

Giuseppe

GIUSEPPE TO LUCREZIA

Rome, 10th November

Yesterday I went to see Ignazio Fegiz, he phoned me and suggested I go to his house to see some paintings by a friend of his. They are pictures of woodland scenes. His flat is small, on a split-level plan with a sitting-room and a room above. I can't bear split-level rooms. I like proper houses with a corridor in them. He has a lot of paintings in the house. I'm not very interested in paintings. I told him so. I also said that he and I perhaps didn't have much to talk about to each other. He said that didn't matter. Two people can get along very well without having anything to talk about. It's true.

In the sitting-room there's a picture of a woman with a great mass of blond hair sitting in an arm-chair. I looked at it and he told me it was a self-portrait by one of his friends. He thought it very beautiful. I'm not so sure. He showed me other pictures by this friend of his. They are mostly landscapes, mainly red and a golden-blond. He looked at the time and said he had to see someone. He couldn't take me home because he was going a different way. We went down together. His house has no lift, there's a rather dirty little flight of stairs. He got into his car, an olive-green Renault. Later Egisto told me that this friend of his, the one with the red and golden-blond paintings, lives in Porta Cavalleggeri and that he eats at her flat almost every evening. Her name is Ippolita, people call her Ippo. She isn't beautiful but she has marvellous thick, curly blond hair. She is very thin. But even though she's so thin she lives in terror of getting fat and eats nothing at all. A bread-stick, a carrot, a lemon. Even so she's a very good cook and invents dishes that she doesn't taste herself. Egisto always knows everyone's business.

Giuseppe

LUCREZIA TO GIUSEPPE

Monte Fermo, 14th November

Yesterday evening the famous Ignazio Fegiz arrived here, famous because you have talked about him so much, and you like him so much, and Egisto also likes him so much, and now Piero too. Albina arrived with Egisto. They came in Ignazio Fegiz's olive-green Renault. They had phoned and we were expecting them. I wanted to make them a meat-loaf but I didn't have time. I'll make one tomorrow. We had eggs and potato soup. The Sicilian general help has disappeared. He took with him some silver tea-spoons, a clock belonging to poor Piero and a tape-recorder. He left early in the morning whilst we were asleep. Poor Piero went to the police. He is especially sorry about the clock because it had a sentimental value for him.

Now I have a great deal to do in the house. The Sicilian didn't do much but at least he swept the rooms clean and washed the vegetables.

Yesterday evening we stayed up till late. Ignazio Fegiz chattered away. How he chatters! He has his say about everything. Art, politics. I fell asleep in a corner of the sofa. I woke up and realized they were talking about you. I shan't tell you what they said. It doesn't seem right to me to tell someone what other people say when he isn't there. Neither the good nor the bad. Not even the good, because then the absence of the words he hasn't heard puff it all up and butter it and sweeten it and make it into something quite different from the truth.

I thought of coming to Rome for a day. But I shan't come. I have too much to do in the house. I will say goodbye to you on this piece of paper.

Your long, thinning hair. Your glasses. Your jumpers with their roll collars, blue in the winter, white in the summer. Your long, bony legs, like a stork's. Your big, long nose, like a stork's. Your big, bony hands that are always cold even when the weather's hot. That's how I remember you.

Lucrezia

GIUSEPPE TO LUCREZIA

Rome, 18th November

My son telephoned from Berlin. He is leaving for Florence. They have decided to shoot some of the film on the hills around Florence. If I came to Florence we could meet. If I come I am to bring a typewriter that he had lent to a friend of his and never got back again. I won't tell you the itinerary Roberta and I had to go through to get hold of that typewriter, in via dei Coronari, then in via dei Giubbonari, tracking down someone called Pino, and then tracking down someone called Mario. We finally found the typewriter with someone called Franca who has a record shop on via Cassia. And it was a wreck.

Roberta, Ignazio Fegiz and I went to Florence. Ignazio Fegiz had to go to Florence too and he took us in his Renault.

Ignazio Fegiz said he had enjoyed himself at *Le Margherite*. He said he slept in a very big, very damp room where there is a chest-of-drawers with tortoises carved on it, and a mirror stained with dark spots. I know that room, I too have slept there so many times. He likes Piero. He said about you that you are a very nervous person, especially at lunch-time when you had made a meat-loaf which fell apart as you were cutting it. He stayed with you for two days and on both days you made a meat-loaf which fell apart. So he asked you why you showed off by making meat-loaves when they were always a failure. You were upset. Piero said that your meat-loaves had a very good taste, even when they fell apart and crumbled like that they were very good. But he said that when a meat-loaf falls apart it is, after all, a failure. That's what he said about you, that you are very nervous, and that your youngest son Vito is extremely spoilt and that at eleven in the evening he is still wandering around the house with a squashed orange in his hand. According to you one shouldn't pass on the things people say about us when we are not there. But I usually pass them on, if they are not really nasty. Perhaps I'm wrong.

We got to Florence late in the evening. Alberico had arranged to meet me at a pensione. They were in the hall, lounging in armchairs, with their rucksacks by their feet. There were three of them, Alberico, a little blond fellow and a tiny girl wearing sky-blue overalls with braces. The little blond fellow was the director of the film, and the girl was the production secretary. The blond fellow's name is Rainer, the girl's name is Nadia. The blond fellow is from Monaco, the girl from Catania. I always feel ill at ease when I find myself face to face with Alberico. I kissed him on his beard. He is taller than I am and I had to stand on tiptoe.

The girl had a splitting headache and she and Roberta went off to find an all-night chemist's. As soon as they had gone Alberico said that the girl was a pain in the neck and the blond fellow said that he thought so too. The blond fellow talked half in German and half in Italian. They had flown to Milan and then come on by train. The girl had been afraid in the plane and the two of them had to take turns to hold her hand. In the train she had been too cold and she had argued with a woman who wanted to turn off the heating. A pain in the neck. All the same, they were tied to her hand and foot because she had put up the money for the film and she would have to put up some more, because if she didn't the film couldn't be finished. She had got them the money from a partner of her father's in Germany because her father had business interests in Germany. Her father is rolling in money. Ignazio Fegiz asked about the film. Alberico said it was a disgusting mess and the blond fellow said he thought so too. Ignazio Fegiz kept asking questions. So they dragged various scribbled notes out of their rucksacks. Ignazio Fegiz tried to go through them but said he found them illegible. Roberta and the girl came back. The girl ordered half a litre of mineral water and a roll. She is a very tiny, plump, pretty girl with a little dark face. She has frizzy, untidy hair, like a black cloud. She has big breasts that seem to be bursting out of her tight overalls.

The following morning Ignazio Fegiz went off on his own business. Roberta and the girl went for a walk through Florence. The blond fellow had got up early and was by this time exploring the hills. Alberico and I had coffee in the hall. I asked him when he was thinking of coming back to Rome, and where he would live seeing that he no longer had a house. I asked him if he still planned to move to the country with Adelmo and raise chickens. He said that he hadn't heard anything from Adelmo for a while and that he didn't think about chickens any more. I said that in that case it would have been better if he hadn't sold his house, however I had made the same mistake too and that we were a couple of idiots to have sold our houses, his and mine. I told him that Roberta would buy me some Treasury Bonds with the money from the sale of my house so that if he ever needed money he could refer to her. He gave a faint smile and said he had plenty of money. When he laughs I feel less ill at ease because I see his little white healthy teeth. I said that in fact he was a rich man. He said that if it came to that I wasn't poor, I was just frightened of becoming poor, a completely different thing from being poor already. I asked him if he would come and see me in America and he said that he might well come over soon, or perhaps next spring.

Everyone came back and we stayed sitting in the hall for a while. Ignazio Fegiz and Roberta talked in German to the blond fellow. I couldn't understand what they were saying but I think they were giving their opinion of the film and offering advice. If Ignazio Fegiz isn't offering advice he isn't happy. Roberta's the same. Just that Roberta's advice tends to be pretty crude, and Ignazio Fegiz's is very affected. The little blond fellow had a bewildered expression on his face. Alberico was reading the newspapers. The girl had ordered a ham roll and was eating it in her secretive, babyish way.

The time for us to leave had come. I kissed Alberico on his beard and for a moment gripped his long cold fingers in my hand. You say that my hands are always cold but you don't know how cold his are.

All three stood on the pavement while were were getting into the car. Alberico was leaning against the wall. He was wearing his tight, short leather coat, his worn-out jeans that are faded at the knee, and filthy white tennis-shoes. The blond fellow had a check flannel shirt on. The girl was eating her ham roll. We left.

Roberta said that she had had a good long chat with the girl while they were wandering through Florence looking at churches. The girl thinks she is pregnant. In Berlin she had an affair with an Austrian journalist. She isn't quite sure that she wants an abortion. The journalist has left Berlin and anyway it wasn't a very close relationship. When she phoned and asked his advice the journalist said she should have an abortion. But she is unsure. Her relationship with her parents is not bad, but not marvellous either. Her parents live near Catania, on their own property. Her father owns a huge construction materials company. He is a millionaire. But she doesn't want to go back to Sicily. When the film is finished she thinks of coming to Rome. Alberico has said he could put her up. Put her up where, said Roberta. Alberico has sold his house and has nowhere to put himself and his own odds and ends. But she said that Alberico knows masses of people in Rome.

We stopped at a motel by the autostrada, to rest and buy biscuits. It was dark when we arrived in Rome. Now I am at home and it is night. This is how my two days, yesterday and today, have been.

Giuseppe

morning, 19th November

Piero phoned me a short while ago and woke me up. He was calling from Perugia, from his office. How early he goes to work, it's only nine. He wanted to say hello to me. He asked me why I didn't come to *Le Margherite* once more before I leave. He asked me not to forget you. I am very fond of Piero. He said that Ignazio Fegiz seemed pleasant enough, but perhaps a little over-critical. I think he found him over-critical about the meat-loaves.

FERRUCCIO TO GIUSEPPE

Princeton, 12th November

My dear Giuseppe,

I would rather phone than write, but when I have phoned you recently I haven't told you something important. I didn't tell you because I find it easier to write it down. The telephone isn't made for saying important things that need time and space, it's made for trivial remarks, or for news that's brief despite its importance.

My dear Giuseppe, I have decided to get married. I am marrying someone I have known for a few years. Her name is Anne Marie Rosenthal. She works with me. I used to think I would never get married, and then all of a sudden I took this decision. Anne Marie is forty-eight, six years younger than me. She came to America during the war. Her father was German and her mother French. Her parents were Jews and her father died in a German concentration camp. She came to America as a child, with her mother and grandmother. She is a widow and has a married daughter who lives in Philadelphia. We decided to get married a month ago during a congress in Philadelphia. I didn't write to you about it earlier because I know your indecisive character and I was afraid my imminent marriage might put you off your plan of coming to stay with me.

You have asked me many times, on the phone and in your letters, if I regretted asking you to come. I don't regret it at all. The three of us – you, Anne Marie and I – shall live very well together. Three is, as you know, a perfect number.

Anne Marie and I are getting married in a week. When you arrive we shall already be married. I shan't wait for you to arrive before I get married, there would be no point. There won't be any kind of celebration.

I shall be in New York at the airport on 30th November to

meet you. Anne Marie will be with me. As you have never seen New York we shall stay there for a week. Then we shall go on to Princeton. As I told you on the phone I've recently moved house. The house I had before was beautiful, this one is less beautiful but more convenient.

With love from

Ferruccio

GIUSEPPE TO PIERO

Rome, 21st November

Thank you for phoning me. I still have your voice ringing in my ears. I am here in my room with my suitcases packed and locked, and bits of paper and string all over the floor.

It would be impossible for me to forget you, and I shall carry all of you – Lucrezia, your dear children – with me in my heart. I shall carry your big, yellow, old house which you call *Le Margherite*, though goodness knows why, with me in my heart. Lucrezia sometimes says she is fed up with that house, she is fed up with living in the country, and wishes you could all move somewhere else. But she is wrong. It is a beautiful house, and you did well to buy it ten years ago, or whenever it was. Stay there. Never leave it.

Yesterday I had a letter from my brother. He says he is getting married. To tell you the truth this news has really worried me. I think I shan't go and live with him. As soon as I have a salary I shall look for a little flat for myself.

I had imagined my brother and me alone, but it won't be like that. That fantasy fell to pieces in less than a moment. And this has made me upset and very worried.

Giuseppe

ALBINA TO GIUSEPPE

Pianura, 22nd November

Dear Giuseppe,

I'm writing to you from the Women's Centre. I'm here with Egisto and Serena. Lucrezia has stayed at home. I'm writing to tell you I can't have supper with you tomorrow evening because I'm staying at Monte Fermo. I couldn't reach you by telephone and I'm sending this letter with the Swiss girl because she will come to Rome tomorrow and she has to bring you a suitcase that you once lent to Piero.

Egisto is banging nails into the stage and Serena is working on her play and banging away at her typewriter so that my head feels as though it's splitting open; I don't know what to do and so I'm writing to you.

Serena has almost finished her play. She is going to act it here in two weeks' time. She will act it alone because there is only one person in her play, Gemma Donati, Dante's wife. No one ever says anything about this Gemma Donati and nothing is known about her. Serena is curious about her precisely because no one talks about her. She sees her as a person who has lost her own identity and who rediscovers it while talking out loud to herself. Serena will be dressed in white and will walk backwards and forwards along the stage holding a book in her hand – the *Divine Comedy* – which she will fling into a fire in a moment of intense rage. In the middle of the stage there will be a brazier with ashes in it, and she will throw the book into the ashes. Serena wanted to make a big blaze with a pile of firewood on the floor, but we forbade her to do this because we were afraid that the whole stage might go up in flames.

Dear Giuseppe, when the Women's Centre opens in two weeks' time, and Serena is Gemma Donati, you will already be no longer in Italy. The costume has been made out of an old sheet and to tell the truth it doesn't suit her very well because it should fall in large folds, and instead it is pretty skimpy, she has cut it all wrong. But she will have some really beautiful gold sandals on and a fillet of gold in her hair.

Dear Giuseppe, how far away you will be in two weeks' time. America is a long way off. It's true that it only takes a day to get there by plane, it's true that everyone comes and goes from America, and it's true that these days distances don't exist any more, but still it's not so easy to come and go around the world if you don't have the money to travel. Egisto says that complaining about distances is part of the past, just as complaining and worrying if someone became ill with tuberculosis is part of the past. In our time distances have disappeared and the fear of tuberculosis has disappeared. Because of aeroplanes and antibiotics these two misfortunes have disappeared. It's true. Even so, neither Egisto nor I have the money to come and see you in America.

On the morning of 30th November, we shall be waiting below your flat with Egisto's Dauphine, and Egisto and I will come to the airport with you.

Albina

GIUSEPPE TO LUCREZIA AND PIERO

New York, 1st December

Dear friends,

I am writing to both of you because I'm thinking of both of you, and because as I left yesterday Egisto gave me that little cheese which he had got from you for me, with your two names written in red on the box. I thank you both.

I am in New York. I arrived all right. I say I arrived all right but to be honest I had a terrible flight. I had a slight sore throat when we left Rome and during the flight this sore throat got worse and I developed a fever. A kind Indian sitting next to me realized that I was ill; he called the hostess and got her to give me something to bring the fever down.

I arrived in New York last night. Now it is seven in the morning. I am in bed, in a hotel on Fifth Avenue. My meeting with America was not a happy one. The high fever I was running as I descended from the plane with the Indian, who carried my bag for me, meant that I wasn't aware of anything. I walked with everyone else along a covered ramp that went on and on for ever. Then I remember everything got very confused, but the Indian was with me all the time. You see, Lucrezia, one always finds protectors. The Indian stayed with me until he saw me meet my brother. Then he gave me my bag and left. I shall never see him again. When I saw my brother's grey loden overcoat in front of me, I felt immensely relieved. His strong presence, and his long, serious face gave me a profound sensation of peace. I embraced him and rested my chest against his coat which was soaking wet from the rain. Behind him there was a short, thin woman with very large, grey, clear, slightly squinting eyes, a cap pulled down over one ear, and a smile. When she turned round I saw that her hair was done in an old-fashioned way, with a bun on the nape of her neck, a big black bun stuffed full of hairpins. Anne Marie.

We took a taxi. I sat between the two of them. There was a travelling rug in the taxi and Anne Marie put it over my knees. My brother said, 'I don't think it's anything. Just an ordinary attack of tonsilitis.'

There were lots of brightly lit underpasses, I saw nothing else. It was pouring down when we got out of the car. Anne Marie covered my head with one of her scarves. There's always someone to protect you. The hotel had a revolving door, and we entered a large hall full of people and suitcases. My brother went up in the lift with me. Her took off his loden overcoat in the room, sat down, and told me to have a shower. But I felt so ill that I undressed and went to bed without even washing my hands. Anne Marie came with an Italian doctor she had found in the hotel. The doctor examined me. I had a fever of 40°. But the doctor too said it was just tonsilitis. Anne Marie went out with the doctor and my brother and I were left alone. He arranged my bedclothes then sat stroking my hair and cheeks. He has a long face with two deep wrinkles down his cheeks, and his forehead is furrowed with horizontal wrinkles; he has thick eyebrows and smooth, tidy grey hair. We don't look like each other. He seems older and looks like my father, whereas I look like my mother.

He decided to get married in Philadelphia, in a Natural History Museum. There was a congress in Philadelphia. He, Anne Marie and the other participants in the congress were taking a walk through the town during a break in the proceedings. It was raining and they all went into the museum. He and Anne Marie soon became separated from the others, and so they were alone. They spent a long time looking at condors, eagles and kangaroos. Then they sat on a bench because it was still raining outside. They had known each other for some time, they worked together, but they had never talked to each other for very long and they knew little about each other. That day they talked for a long time. They discussed everything under the sun. When they came out he had decided to marry her and he told her the following day and she agreed.

Anne Marie came to America as a child, with her mother. They had no money. Her mother supported her while she was studying by working as a cashier in a restaurant. When she was eighteen she married a sculptor from Alsace. Her mother had been against this marriage and broke off relations with her. The sculptor became an alcoholic and treated her badly. She had a baby girl and her mother died. She separated from her husband who killed himself a short time afterwards. Her daughter is thirty now; she is married and works in an advertising agency.

Anne Marie is a calm person with simple habits. She speaks three languages fluently – French, German and English. She doesn't know Italian. She intends to learn. She enjoys cooking and doing embroidery. She plays the piano. But her real love is scientific research. This is how my brother described her to me while he was walking up and down the room. I just wanted to hide my head under the bedclothes and go to sleep.

Anne Marie came back with a little teapot. There is a small electric stove in the room. Anne Marie made me some mint tea which I drank. Mint tea seems to be one of her obsessions. They went off and I was finally able to get to sleep. During the night I woke up every now and then, and the fever, the mint tea, the sculptor from Alsace and the Natural History Museum became confused in my head, as if they were a slimy mess in which I was exhaustedly splashing about.

Now it's morning. I still have a fever. I am writing to you in bed. I feel terrible. But, as my brother and the doctor say, it's nothing. It's just ordinary tonsilitis.

Giuseppe

PIERO TO GIUSEPPE

Perugia, 13th December

Dear Giuseppe,

I'm writing to you from Perugia; I'm here in my office. My partner, Doctor Corsi, has already gone. It's eight in the evening and now I shall go home too. The road is foggy and I shall have to go very slowly. Sometimes I wish I had a house in Perugia. Lucrezia wants that very much. She'd like to live in Rome even more. But, as you say, it would be a mistake. It's lovely to wake up in the morning in the country, with the cocks crowing and the birdsong and the good smell of the air. I'm sure that these things are important to Lucrezia too, and that if we lived in Perugia or Rome she would be unhappy.

I will send this to Princeton, because Roberta told us that she talked on the phone to your brother and that you are about to leave New York. She told us that you are over your tonsilitis now and that you are feeling better.

Lucrezia and I read your letter by the fire, we were eating chestnuts. We phoned Roberta the following day. She reassured us about your health.

Look, you mustn't take your brother's marriage the way you are doing. It's not the end of the world for goodness sake. It's nothing extraordinary, nothing special. Whilst we were reading your letter Lucrezia shrugged her shoulders and snorted with exasperation. She said that when you have a bit of a fever you get it into your head that you have God knows what terrible disease, and she said that you are a tremendous egotist because if your brother gets married and is happy then you ought to be happy for him and instead you carry on as if you had landed in the middle of some appalling disaster. Then Serena came and felt sorry for you in America with a fever and the mint tea and Anne Marie.

It certainly is strange that your brother decided to get married now of all times, just when you had decided to go and live with him. It's strange, but these things happen and I don't see why you have to talk about it in such a miserable way.

Anne Marie will keep house. It's true that you're very good at keeping house too, but perhaps Anne Marie will be even better at it than you. From what you say of her, she is a woman who has had a hard life and a hard life makes people want order; it makes them care about the little things that contribute to their own and others' comfort. Lucrezia thinks this is not true and we talked it over, but I stick to my opinion.

We all miss you very much and we remember when you read Plato's *Dialogues* to us. At the moment we have to listen to Serena's play which to tell you the truth seems to me to be a load of rubbish – I don't know if you know that she is Gemma Donati, Dante's wife. When she is Gemma Donati and walks backwards and forwards in the dining room reading from her sheets of paper, the children hide behind the sofas and then suddenly leap out and squirt her with their water-pistols. But she continues as if nothing were happening. Poor Serena, the fact is she needs a man because she doesn't have a very cheerful life in that room in Pianura, it's always in such a terrible mess; she's not someone who knows how to keep things in order, her room is always piled high with books, newspapers and jumpers. Poor Serena, poor Gemma Donati without a Dante, without even a real talent for the theatre and by now getting on for thirty-nine. Her father is always writing to her saying that she should leave Pianura and that he doesn't understand why she has hidden herself away in Pianura just to be near us and that we won't be there for her to lean on for ever. I thought that perhaps Ignazio Fegiz might become the man in her life but Lucrezia says no, because he just demolishes her and that once when she was reading her play he told her that she read badly and that her accent was too Piemontese for Dante's wife (and in fact she was born in Limone, in Piedmont). Then the two of them started an interminable discussion about the theatre and dialects and everything – enough to make anyone die of boredom.

I will say goodbye now because it is getting really late and when I'm late Lucrezia worries and goes out on to the terrace to watch the road.

Piero

EGISTO AND ALBINA TO GIUSEPPE

Rome, 16th December

Dear Giuseppe,

We are writing you this letter together, we are in Albina's room sitting on the sofa, she has the typewriter on her knees, one of us says one phrase and the other another. We've eaten boiled eggs and tinned beans. We think of you. Come back here. We heard from Piero and Lucrezia that you have had a fever and you feel miserable and your brother has got married; goodness only knows what you think you're doing in America.

It will be Christmas soon and you remember that last year we all spent Christmas and the New Year together at *Le Margherite* and we were pretty cheerful. This year we shall go to *Le Margherite* again for Christmas and the New Year but you won't be there. Ignazio Fegiz will be there and in a way he has taken your place, in the sense that he comes often and that they make a great fuss of him. But we liked you better because we have known you for such a long time and also because you have a much sweeter disposition; he is one of those people who have to argue and get worked up and shout.

Last Friday the Women's Centre opened with Serena's play, which is called *Gemma and the Flames*. Serena's father made a special trip from Genoa. He is a large, old man with a big white moustache. He sat in the front row between Piero and Lucrezia. There were people from Pianura, among the ladies there was the chemist, the tobacconist and the two who keep the electrical goods shop in the square, a few men, about twenty people altogether. The tickets were free. It went on for a long time and our feet were cold, but it was a success because everyone stayed quiet and attentive – as if they felt a bit intimidated – and at the end they clapped a lot. Serena was happy and bright red in the face, in her sheet. They put her father up at *Le Margherite,* in the room which has the chest of drawers with the tortoises carved on it, and the mirror with the dark stains. It's the best room. Lucrezia had made him a big dinner with roast chickens, salads and vegetable pies. She wanted to make a meat-loaf but Piero didn't let her because her meat-loaves fall apart, as you know. Piero is under some obligation to Serena's father because it was he who found him that job in Perugia in Doctor Corsi's office all those years ago. Now Piero and Doctor Corsi have become partners. Doctor Corsi came to the dinner, and also to the performance. Ignazio Fegiz was at the dinner but he didn't come to the play; he said he had a headache and stayed behind at the house. Under his breath he told us that he didn't want to know anything about Dante's wife. He preferred Dante. Usually he sleeps in the room with the tortoises, but this time they gave him the little room on the top floor, the one where there are quilts with dragons on them.

Goodbye, we shall stop this letter because we realize we are just piling up pointless details.

Egisto and Albina

GIUSEPPE TO LUCREZIA

Princeton, 24th December

I have been in Princeton for a fortnight. I have had a letter from Piero and one from Egisto and Albina together. I haven't had so much as a line from you. I wish you a Happy Christmas.

Princeton is a very small town, very beautiful, full of parks. It is cut down the middle by a street called Nassau Street. From my window I can see parks, little houses, and trees with the famous squirrels that you were so curious about. My room is on the ground floor. The wallpaper has flying bear-cubs on it, every bear-cub has a red balloon. It was evidently the children's room when the previous occupants were here. My brother said that he hadn't had time to change the wallpaper. I said I didn't mind, though to tell the truth I'd have preferred it if he had had it changed. It's a two-storey house. My brother and Anne Marie sleep upstairs. She has left the flat she used to have and has had her furniture – which includes an armchair that has been put in my room – brought here. It's the one I'm sitting in at the moment, as I write. I have a sofa-bed to sleep on. It was a little difficult for me to open and close it at first, but I have learnt how to do it now.

I am in good health. I spend hours every day in my room. I have started to write a novel. I used to write novels when I was twenty. I never finished any of them. Perhaps I shall manage to finish this one. My brother and Anne Marie don't know that I am writing a novel. I told them I was writing a paper on Flaubert.

I write in longhand, sitting in an armchair with a large book on my knees and the paper resting on the book. I have never liked typing. True, I used to write articles on the typewriter, but when I write anything else, anything that is not meant for the newspapers, I prefer to use a ballpoint pen. But generally speaking I have kept very little of the things that I have written in ballpoint throughout my life. When I re-read them I felt uncomfortable and tore them up. Now I would like to see if I can manage to write something I shan't tear up.

I wake up early in the morning. Before I get up I stare for a long time at the bear-cubs and the balloons. Then I go into the kitchen and make myself a coffee. Anne Marie comes in a little later, in her dressing-gown, and she starts to make the breakfast for my brother and herself. She heats up the milk, toasts the bread, beats the eggs. In the morning she doesn't have her hair in a bun, instead it is gathered in a long plait. She smiles all the time. She smiles with her mouth, but her eyes and the rest of her face don't smile. She and I sometimes talk to one another in English and sometimes in French, but we have nothing to say to each other in any language. Then my brother appears from the bathroom in his striped dressing-gown. They have a long, careful breakfast, which I don't take part in but at which I am present. When they have finished breakfast I help Anne Marie to wash the dishes. I take the rubbish bags to the dustbin which is in front of the door. And here's my brother in his loden overcoat and Anne Marie with her bun. Anne Marie puts her cap on in front of the hall mirror, and tilts it over one ear. They take their bicycles out of the garage and go off to the Institute. I wave to them from the window. I am alone.

I don't go out much. During the first days I was here I went out with my brother a few times. They were the only times in which he and I were together without Anne Marie, and I anxiously searched around inside myself for things to say to him, without finding a single phrase. He was a bit embarrassed, too. Perhaps he thinks that I don't like Anne Marie. It's true, I can't stand her; I can't stand either her long neck, or her clear squinting eyes, or her smile, or her plait, or her bun. But I can't tell him that and I'm unable to tell him anything else. When I'm alone I don't want to go out, I don't feel any great curiosity to go and look around, I feel that I'm neither a visitor passing through nor an inhabitant of the place; I'm someone who doesn't know what to be and who stares at everything indecisively.

Anne Marie and my brother come back at seven in the evening. Anne Marie immediately starts cooking. She cooks very complicated dishes, slices of meat with minced carrots, beetroot and cabbage mixed up together, sauces with flour and cream. Since I have been here she has never made a meat-loaf but I'm sure that if she did make one it wouldn't fall apart. She hurries about the kitchen darting that long neck of hers this way and that, smiling the whole time. I offer to help her. She politely refuses. My brother and I sit in the living-room and wait for supper to be ready. He reads scientific journals and I read detective stories. Every now and then he raises his head and asks me if what I am reading is interesting. I always say yes. I look at him. As I look at him, whilst he is reading seated at the table, with his chin cupped in his hand and his wrinkled forehead, I experience once again the feeling of great calm that he always used to give me when we were children, and when I thought of him in Italy. He has always been a secure point of reference for me, a tree-trunk I could lean against, someone from whom I could at every moment ask for explanations, judgements, reproaches and absolution. But in fact I never ask him for anything now. Our relationship has been interrupted. It seems to me that he doesn't have space for me now. After the evening of my arrival he has said nothing more to me about his marriage. And whilst I look at him I feel that behind his authoritative appearance an extreme embarrassment, as far as I am concerned, is hiding itself – a dislike even, a disgust, which is not at all severe or condemnatory, but simply irritated. We go and sit down to supper. I don't like Anne Marie's soups at all but I eat them all the same and praise them to the skies in French and in English. At table my brother and Anne Marie hold hands. They drink milk and fruit juices. Towards evening I always go to the 'Wines and Spirits' and buy myself a can of beer. They could remember at least once that I drink beer and buy some for me. They don't do so. They don't remember. It will seem silly to you, but this upsets me.

Sometimes two of my brother's friends come over after supper. Their names are Schultz and Kramer. They work in the same Institute. My brother and Anne Marie talk and laugh a lot with them, until late at night. I stay for a while during these conversations, without understanding anything because they are on scientific subjects and because I don't know English well enough. I go to bed early.

I had an interview for an Italian teaching post. They accepted me. I shall teach Italian in a school. A few days ago my brother and I went to see the director. I start at the beginning of January.

My brother has advised me to buy a bicycle. I shall cycle to school. According to my brother you enjoy the fresh morning air better on a bicycle than on foot.

I shall teach for two or three months or so and then perhaps I shall return to Italy. Goodness only knows why I was such an idiot as to sell my house.

Giuseppe

Anne Marie's daughter and son-in-law have arrived. They are sleeping in the drawing room where there are two sofa-beds. They will spend the New Year here. The daughter is a thin, skinny girl. She wears spectacles and she's pregnant. The son-in-law is a little fellow, thin, with red hair and jug ears. The son-in-law's name is Danny, the daughter's Chantal. They both work in an advertising agency.

I've bought a bicycle.

ROBERTA TO ALBERICO

Rome, 15th January

Dear Alberico,

I was very pleased that you phoned me yesterday, and I thank you very much for your New Year's greetings, even though I realize that you didn't phone to wish me a Happy New Year but for your own purposes. You asked me to find you a house to rent in Rome, and you want it at once, by the end of the month. My dear boy, if you think it is easy to find a house in Rome you are mistaken. You say you want it to be central, really central, in old Rome; poor boy if you think it is easy to find a house to rent in old Rome you have another think coming.

Your flat in via Torricelli was not in old Rome, but it was a splendid flat. You made a terrible mistake when you sold it, and your father made a terrible mistake too when he sold his flat here, above me, where the Lanzaras are now. You have been a couple of real fools.

I've asked someone I know who has an estate agent's to look out for a house for you wherever possible.

You told me you have also phoned your father recently, and that was very good of you. You get in touch so seldom that every sign of life you give is all to the good.

I also phoned your father over the New Year. He seemed to me to be in a very bad mood. When I phoned there were guests in the house, your Uncle Ferruccio's wife's daughter and son-in-law. The house was probably in something of a muddle and your father detests muddle, and he doesn't like guests in the house as you know. And perhaps he doesn't like your uncle's wife, this Anne Marie woman, much. That's the impression I got. He doesn't like America at all either, though what's he seen of it? He hasn't seen anything, in New York he had a bit of a sore throat and stayed holed up in his hotel, and now he's in Princeton he's always shut up in the house – from what he told me – even if he hasn't got a sore throat any more. He's a real character your father is.

I spent New Year's Eve upstairs in the flat that used to be your father's. The Lanzaras invited me. The flat is still a bit disorganized because they only moved in a few days ago. They have made some changes and it's unrecognizable, but in those places where I did recognise it I felt very sad, because I remembered when I used to come up and find your father there and now I find the Lanzaras instead. They are kind, pleasant people, but you can well understand how it's not the same for me.

They have made a lot of changes. They have given those pale blue kitchen fittings to the caretaker and they've made a new kitchen with co-ordinated units. To tell the truth I'd have been grateful if they'd given them to me, but apparently it didn't occur to them. It's a pity your father didn't think of giving them to me, seeing that the Lanzaras didn't want them – I suppose they thought them old-fashioned and not very stylish.

Anyway, I had a really lively New Year's Eve with the Lanzaras. I took two pies up, one cheese and one vegetable, and I gave up my diet for the evening; there were lots of different dishes and I tried them all. I think you should be psychoanalysed by Tonino Lanzara. He is a good analyst, he's very serious and you need an analyst. You need one, let me tell you, you need one as much as you need bread to eat.

I don't want to lecture you because that's not how I am, but when you come back to Rome try not to spend time in all those awful places. When you were here you got into awful habits, so much so that you finished up in jail; be careful that doesn't happen to you again.

I can well believe that you haven't finished the film, but I'm sorry. Anyway, it's been an experience for you, and perhaps you will be able to continue working in the cinema.

I would like news of that girl Nadia whom you introduced me to in Florence that day. I'd like to know if she had an abortion or not. You say I'm to find a flat for you and for your friends. I'd like to know if these friends are the same as the ones I met that day.

With love from

Roberta

Your father has bought a bicycle. The only thing he's managed to do since he arrived in America is to buy himself a bicycle.

GIUSEPPE TO ROBERTA

Princeton, 18th January

Dear Roberta,

I was really pleased to hear your voice when you phoned a few days ago with your best wishes for the New Year. Then Piero and Lucrezia phoned too from Monte Fermo, and Egisto, Serena, Albina, all our friends, they were all there together, and I think Ignazio Fegiz was there too, or at least there was a voice that seemed like his. When they phoned it was late at night because they had mixed up the time difference and they thought it was day time over here. Anne Marie came down in her nightdress to answer the phone. She has a pink flannel nightdress. There were lots of voices on the phone and I realized they were snatching the receiver from each other to say something to me, and then they were laughing and shrieking – they must have had quite a lot of wine to drink. For a moment Lucrezia's voice was there too, but only for a moment. It was a real joy for me to hear all their voices together and to think of them all together there, at *Le Margherite*, in the sitting-room, that sitting-room I remember so well with the big oval table, the lamp-shade with its frayed border, the basket of firewood and the dogs' cushion, the sofa in front of the fireplace, and over the fireplace the picture of King Lear.

I start my lessons in two days, I'm not excited about it. I just have to teach Italian literature to a class of thirty people, all adults. I'm not worried. I'm pleased that I'll have an income. I shall go every morning at nine. I shall go by bicycle. Ferruccio has shown me the road I have to take.

When I was young I taught history and philosophy in high schools. It's strange that here in America I should go back to doing those things I did when I was young; writing a novel, cycling, teaching.

After the New Year Anne Marie's daughter and son-in-law left. This was a relief to me because the house had been in a muddle and because the son-in-law often came and sat in my room, why I don't know. I think he felt that he liked me. He is someone who is full of problems. He has difficulties at work and his relationship with his wife is not an easy one. He suffers from insomnia. He lost his father and mother, and he had an unhappy childhood, tossed backwards and forwards, entrusted to different families that for one reason or another he had to leave. He would like his wife to be kinder to him. His wife has a strong, arrogant nature. That's what he claims. I said I didn't see all this strength and arrogance in Chantal. She seems a gentle girl. She used to appear in the kitchen in the mornings, with her pregnant belly, her glasses, her dishevelled hair about her neck, in a cheap grey woollen dress with four big buttons down one side of her belly and four down the other, with an air of being serious, determined, deep in thought. Every now and again though she would give a shrill, unexpected burst of laughter, like the shrieking of some bird, when she upset the milk or burnt the toast. Danny told me that she and her mother do not see eye to eye. Anne Marie is also a strong, arrogant woman. I finally realized why Danny came and sat in my room. Because he couldn't stand Anne Marie and he had realized that I couldn't stand her either.

Danny must be about Alberico's age, or a few years older. Like Alberico he had a difficult childhood. Alberico wasn't tossed backwards and forwards because there was always Aunt Bice. But he too experienced little or no happiness while he was a child. Everywhere you look you find difficult childhoods, insomnia, neuroses, problems.

I think I'll return to Italy in a few months. I thought I'd stay here till June and then return. You will have to help me find a house. I haven't talked about it to Ferruccio. I'll tell him when it's convenient. Selling my house was certainly a big mistake. You were right. Never mind, what's done can't be undone and there's a reason for everything. A stupid proverb because the things we do often have neither rhyme nor reason to them. Remember me to the Lanzaras. Sometimes I hate them because they are in my house. That house will always be mine, even if I have sold it to the Lanzaras. Remember me to the walls of my house, to the convent garden, to the newspaper kiosk, to the Mariuccia Restaurant and to the Café Esperia.

Alberico phoned me. He told me he will go back to Italy at the end of the month. I imagine that he will have to look for a house too.

Giuseppe

ROBERTA TO ALBERICO

Rome, 23rd January

Dear Alberico,

Egisto has told me that there is an empty flat under his. The previous tenant left a few days ago. I don't know if you can remember who Egisto is. He is a friend of your father's, and also of mine. A journalist. He lives in Piazza San Cosimato. I met him in the street this morning. He told me about the flat and I phoned the landlady. Then I went there and I think she must have liked me because she immediately agreed to show me the flat. I immediately offered to pay her two months' rent. I went to the bank to withdraw the cash and I took it over to her.

I phoned you before I went to the bank but I couldn't get hold of you. I had to hurry and I thought it best to come to an agreement without asking you. The flat has four rooms. There are some loose tiles and the fittings are shabby, but I don't think that will worry you. It costs four hundred thousand lire a month. That's more than it's worth but not too much more. You can give me the money I've paid in advance when you come.

I hope you haven't changed your mind in the meantime. If you have changed your mind let me know at once. And in any case let me know the date of your arrival. I have the keys.

Roberta

To be honest with you, as soon as he had told me about the flat Egisto rather regretted that he'd done so, probably because he remembered that you had been in prison, and the various things people say about you. He was afraid that you might make him appear in a bad light with his landlady. He started to say that the flat was tiny and too expensive and dark. But I didn't pay any attention. I had to drag the landlady's number out of him. He couldn't retreat any further. On the other hand he's a trustworthy person and as he will have the flat above yours you'll be able to ask him to do lots of things for you.

ALBERICO TO ROBERTA

Berlin, 28th January

Dear Roberta,

As I told you on the phone yesterday everything's fine with me. Thanks very much, as always you've been marvellous. I can't remember this Egisto fellow. I shall arrive at the beginning of February. I will phone you. Piazza San Cosimato will be fine for me. It's not in old Rome, it's part of Trastevere, but it's just as good.

Nadia hasn't had an abortion. She's still pregnant. She will have the child in April. She's an idiot, but she hangs on to me for dear life and I can't get rid of her, and anyway she will pay half the rent. There will be three of us in the flat – me, Nadia, and an Italian boy I've met here who is called Salvatore. Don't worry, I will pay you back the money as soon as possible.

I shall come to collect the keys.

Alberico

ROBERTA TO ALBERICO

Rome, 29th January

My Dear Alberico,

Something terrible has happened. Your Uncle Ferruccio has died. He died in Princeton, of cerebral thrombosis, whilst giving a paper at a conference. Your father and Anne Marie, your uncle's wife – whom I've never met – were in the audience. They realized that he was having difficulty talking, and then they saw him turn pale and fall. He died a little later in hospital, without having regained consciousness.

Your father phoned me from the hospital. He seemed shattered. I told him I'd leave for America immediately. I called you but you were out. I left my number but you didn't call back. I sent you a telegram. I'm leaving. See if you can't come too.

Roberta

PIERO AND LUCREZIA TO GIUSEPPE

Monte Fermo, 29th January

Dear Giuseppe,

Roberta phoned us a short while ago. We have heard your terrible news. I remember your brother well. I met him in Rome last year. We ate in a restaurant on via Cassia. I was there, you, Lucrezia, and perhaps Roberta. Your brother and I had a long, pleasant conversation. About America, Italy, the contemporary world. He was a very intelligent, cultured man. I realize that his death will be a great loss to you. You have not been there long. He had not been married long. A sad fate. Roberta cried when she phoned us. She's on her way. She is a woman who is always ready to run to wherever she's needed. She will be a comfort to you.

Lucrezia and I feel very close to you. We send you our best love. Lucrezia wants to add a couple of words.

Piero

Dear Giuseppe,

Come back. Do everything quickly and come back. We are waiting for you. You can stay at your cousin's. Or you can come and stay with us, at Monte Fermo, for a while. The main thing is that you come away soon. What can you do there now? Your cousin will come and you must return with her, at once.

Lucrezia

ALBINA TO SERENA

Luco dei Marsi 8th February

My dear Serena.

I am at Luco dei Marsi because my mother has broken her femur. I asked for a week's leave from school. There's no telephone at my family's house here. You can imagine how cheerful it is for me to be here, with no telephone, with my irritable mother, Maura and Gina being no help, my father who is getting deafer and deafer, my brother who wants his shirts ironed. I fling his shirts back at him, and then he becomes like a wild animal and the house is full of endless shouting.

You will have heard that Giuseppe's brother has died. Egisto told me when I phoned him from a public call-box. I remember the morning Giuseppe left. He was in a real state. He had a sore throat. His brother had written telling him that he had got married. This was worrying him. We went to the airport with him, me, his cousin Roberta, and Egisto. He isn't the sort to move from one continent to another. He's the sort for a sedentary life. He's afraid of everything. He went to America in order to hide himself away under his brother's wings. But brothers don't have wings. Once you've reached a certain age you realize that either you stand on your own two feet, or you've had it. Giuseppe reached that age some time ago. But he has those long, skinny legs that hold him up so badly. He still has a craving to be protected. Perhaps he didn't have enough affection when he was a child. But then which of us hasn't suffered from lack of affection. I have. And you have too. In fact the affection we are given is always less than we need. Giuseppe went to America in order to feel more protected. Just ask yourself what kind of a reason that is for going to America. You go to America out of a spirit of adventure. He was the opposite. Anyway, when he gets there his brother dies. Now he will come back again.

Dear Serena, I get the impression that Lucrezia has fallen in love with Ignazio Fegiz, and perhaps he has with her. To tell you the truth, from the first few times that he came to *Le Margherite* I thought this would happen. I sense it immediately when something starts to go on between two people. I feel the air becoming warm and light. But in this case I also felt there was something uneasy and fearful between them. I couldn't tell you why. I find Ignazio Fegiz handsome, but I don't like him. Once he told me I act too much like a young girl, and that I dress too much like a young girl, and that there is nothing worse than a thirty-year-old woman who behaves and dresses like a girl and has a lined, tired face. This was a horrible thing to do, and he said it just like that, quietly, tapping my hand as he did so. I felt absolutely terrible. He realized and perhaps he was sorry because later in the evening, when I played the flute, he said that I played well. Nevertheless, he had really hurt me and for days I felt bad about my face, and there's nothing worse than thinking about your own face constantly, hating it and avoiding all the mirrors.

I'll stop now, Serena; write to me here at Luco, where I'm bored stiff. Give me your news, and news of Lucrezia, of everyone. And I'd like to know if you read your poetry at the Women's Centre as you wanted to. Write to me, because I don't have anyone to talk to here, and a letter would be company for me.

Albina

SERENA TO ALBINA

Pianura, 10th February

Dear Albina,

You've got hold of some crazy ideas in Luco dei Marsi. Lucrezia is not in love with Ignazio Fegiz and he is not in love with her. I have never suffered from a lack of affection. In fact I even had too much affection when I was a child. Giuseppe didn't go to America to be protected by his brother but for a much simpler reason, he didn't have any money here, or it seemed to him that he had very little. His brother told him that he could teach in America. They pay teachers well in America. And now his brother is dead. I didn't like his brother. He thought too much of himself. But when someone dies you immediately start to think of him with respect and admiration even if you didn't like him, goodness knows why. It's not as if death were something meritorious. It comes to everyone sooner or later.

I haven't read my poems at the Women's Centre and perhaps I never shall. I bet no one comes on Friday evening. I've lost heart. Last Friday only two turned up. There were precisely two, the chemist and a boy, the caretaker's son. We played records. I danced with the boy. I closed the place at ten.

I don't like Ignazio Fegiz. I don't find him handsome, and I don't even find him particularly intelligent. He has a girl friend he's very attached to. She is rather ugly, with beautiful hair. I know because various people have told me. She is on drugs, they say. He and I argue furiously with one another. When I know he is at *Le Margherite* I don't go, I stay in Pianura. I eat something in my room. I curl up in bed and read. At the moment I like being alone. Being alone doesn't suit everyone. It doesn't suit you because you think about things which exist neither in this world nor the next. But being alone suits me and I like it.

Yours

Serena

GIUSEPPE TO LUCREZIA

Princeton, 14th February

My Lucrezia,

I received Piero's letter and your few, quick words. You tell me to come back at once. I can't. There are so many things that have to be done here, business that has to be finished off. And I can't leave Anne Marie alone at the moment.

Tell Piero I'll write to him soon.

Roberta left a few days ago. Yesterday Danny and Chantal left. They are Anne Marie's son-in-law and daughter. They live in Philadelphia. I don't know whether I've written to you about them. They slept in the sitting-room, Roberta slept in a little room which is used for storing suitcases.

Yesterday we packed up all my brother's clothes and odds and ends and sent them to a home for the blind. One of our neighbours, Mrs Mortimer, helped us. She phoned the home. She is very kind and has been a great help to us.

Roberta was a great help to us too, while she was here. Chantal is eight months pregnant and mustn't tire herself. Danny is someone who's full of problems. And so Roberta and Mrs Mortimer had to think of everything.

Roberta is someone who makes friends with everyone and she immediately made friends with Danny and Chantal. This Danny constantly needs to talk about his problems with someone. He would sit himself down in front of Roberta with a glass of whisky and talk to her about himself till two in the morning. Roberta is very patient and she stayed and listened to him. I don't have her kind of patience. When he planted himself in front of me I sent him about his business.

Now Anne Marie and I have been left alone. She is a strong woman, but she's tired and needs me. And in a way I need her too. I'm very tired too.

The thought that relations were so cold between me and my

brother during those last days won't leave me alone. To be honest they were cold from the first day I arrived here. So many times he came and asked me to go for a walk with him and I refused to. What wouldn't I give to have him in front of me now, to stand up and follow him. I used to refuse coldly, and perhaps rather rudely. It even happened the day before he died. And when I did agree to go out with him we used to walk along exchanging a few cold words with one another. I have to go back years and years before I can rediscover a happy intimate relationship between us.

Yesterday Anne Marie and I went to the cemetery. I took her arm. She cried, but she doesn't stop smiling even when she cries. It's a smile that doesn't reach either her cheeks or her eyes, it stays fixed between her chin and her lips. When we got back to the house I sat in the kitchen, she came and stood beside me and stroked my head. Then I rested my head against her, against the black woollen dress she was wearing over her thin belly. She made me some mint tea, that damned mint tea that she is obsessed with. Then we reheated and ate a bit of roast that Mrs Mortimer had cooked. Anne Marie sat opposite me and ate – self-possessed, dressed in black, with her long neck, her slender shoulders, her smile. Anne Marie and I never talk about my brother. We talk about day-to-day things, the shopping, the washing-machine, Mrs Mortimer, and we talk about Danny's problems and Chantal's character. We don't have many things to talk about, except these which however are soon exhausted. But Ignazio Fegiz once said to me that it's not important to have something to talk about – two people can stay together without having anything special to say to each other and without looking for something, each immersed in his own thoughts, in silence.

Sometimes those friends of my brother's, Schultz and Kramer, come and see us in the evening. Anne Marie talks to them about scientific subjects and things to do with the Institute. I stay quiet. When they go I walk to the gate with them, and at the same time take the rubbish out. Anne Marie hasn't started work again at the Institute yet, but she will do in a few days. And I shall start my lessons at the school again in a few days. Perhaps, I'm not sure, I'll start work again on that thing I've been writing. But at the moment I'm unable to do anything. I spend hours sitting in an armchair in my room staring at the bear-cubs. But I leave the door open and watch Anne Marie who knits in the sitting-room. Mrs Mortimer told her that when things are difficult knitting is a great comfort.

Giuseppe

ALBERICO TO GIUSEPPE

Rome, 20th February

Respected father,

I have been in Rome for a week. I stayed with Roberta, who had just returned from America. I'm sorry about your brother. I saw him three times in all. Once when I was little, in my grandparents' house, and the other two times in your house. He told me to study civil engineering all three times, and all three times I told him I had other plans. Though to be honest I've changed these plans continually over the years. At the present moment I don't have any.

Roberta has found me a flat. Someone called Egisto, whom I think you know, lives on the floor above. He's a short, squat, dark chap. He has come down two or three times and asked me if I needed anything. We needed some bouillon cubes and he brought me some. There are three of us in the flat; me, Nadia, Salvatore. You know Nadia, you saw her that day in Florence. She's pregnant. Roberta told me that you also have a pregnant girl in the house, in Princeton. Nadia is an idiot. She uses her pregnancy as an excuse to do nothing but read magazines. Salvatore and I do the shopping and cook, and we have started to paint all the rooms white. Salvatore is a graphic artist. But he hasn't any work and he's looking for some. We met in Berlin, in a Chinese restaurant.

Roberta suggested that I come to America with her, but I didn't come, I thought I'd probably just be in your way.

With love from

Alberico

GIUSEPPE TO ALBERICO

Princeton, 27th February

Dear Alberico,

You address me as 'respected father' as if I were a priest. However I'm grateful to you for your letter. I haven't had many from you, in your life. I will keep this one in my wallet, next to my heart, like something rare and precious.

You write 'If I'd come, I would have just been in your way'. I stopped and thought for a while about that 'just'. I asked myself if you really believe that a meeting with you would give me nothing but the feeling that you were in the way.

I had Anne Marie read your letter. She smiled. She really does smile the whole time. Sometimes – very rarely – she turns the corners of her mouth right down. But perhaps you don't know who Anne Marie is. She is my brother's widow. My brother loved her, and as it's turned out, she is the only thing of his I still have.

With love from

your father

ROBERTA TO GIUSEPPE

Rome 29th February

Dear Giuseppe,

As soon as I got back to Rome I phoned you but neither you nor Anne Marie were at home and Mrs Mortimer answered. She said you'd gone out shopping. I didn't phone again but in any case it's often impossible to say anything on the phone.

Alberico is in Rome and he has moved into his flat. Three of them are living together; Alberico, that girl Nadia who is six months pregnant, and a friend of Alberico's called Salvatore. He isn't the child's father. The child's father is a Viennese who is in Vienna and who Nadia has finished with. Salvatore is one of those like your son. He doesn't go out with girls. It seems to me that the three of them get on perfectly. The flat is pretty filthy but Salvatore says he is going to clean it thoroughly. He has a long, bony face, a big black moustache and black side-whiskers. Nadia has a great belly. She wears black silk harem-pants and a sweat-shirt with '*I* want to decide' written on it. She has a little pale face that seems all eyes and hair. She hasn't got anything ready for the baby yet, but a friend has lent them a pram which they keep in the sitting-room and which is at the moment piled high with saucepans. When I saw them, she was stretched out on the sofa reading comics. Her parents send her money but they don't want her in Sicily. Your son was typing, he's writing the screen-play for a film. Salvatore was doing the ironing. In the flat there's a typewriter, an ironing-board, a table, some beds and a telly. The clothes are all piled up on a bed they are not using.

Now I'll talk to you about yourself. I'd like you to tell me what you intend doing, because I asked you in Princeton but you always answered vaguely. I imagine you will come back to live in Rome. I don't think you will want to stay in America now that you no longer have your brother there. And so I'll have to find you a flat. As for the money, well you've been fretting over this recently but that's just self-indulgence, you have land in Puglia that you could sell for a pretty good price. With the money from the flat you sold you could buy another flat – much smaller and much worse than the other one of course. Those fine Lanzaras led you up the garden path. Enough. We all make mistakes. Anyway, let me know what you plan to do.

With love from

Roberta

LUCREZIA TO GIUSEPPE

Monte Fermo, 5th March

Dear Giuseppe,

I received your letter and it has made me very melancholy. I don't understand why you don't say when you intend to come back. I phoned Roberta and she told me that she doesn't know either. You wanted to live with your brother but now he is dead, so whatever are you doing there?

You talk a lot about Anne Marie and Mrs Mortimer and other people I don't know and never will know. I don't understand why you don't just leave them all to stew in their own juice.

Ignazio Fegiz came and I told him about your letter. It had really chilled me, made my soul feel stone-cold, and I had to talk to someone about the cold feeling it had given me. We went for a long walk with the children and when we came back it was dark. Piero and Egisto came out with torches to meet us. Piero had become worried when he didn't see us coming back.

I don't like writing 'Ignazio Fegiz' because I don't like the name Ignazio, and I don't like his surname much either. And so when I mention him in my letters I shall just put the initials 'I.F.'. 'I.F.' sends his regards. He doesn't generally write letters, but perhaps he'll write to you some day.

Lucrezia

GIUSEPPE TO ROBERTA

Princeton, 10th March

Dear Roberta,

You ask me if I want you to find me a flat in Rome. Good God, I don't know. I haven't decided anything.

Thank you for your concern, and for the affection with which you think of me. When I start thinking of coming back I'll write to you. Then will be the time to look for a flat.

Chantal's baby was born yesterday. They've called her Margaret. Danny phoned from the clinic. We will go to Philadelphia to see her within the next few days. I bought a bottle of champagne and a cake. Mrs Mortimer came round too and we celebrated Margaret's birth.

Giuseppe

PIERO TO GIUSEPPE

Perugia, 10th May

Dear Giuseppe,

I heard from Lucrezia that you are not coming back at the moment. I haven't seen your letter to Lucrezia. Lucrezia wouldn't let me read it, as is right seeing that it was addressed only to her. She simply told me that for the moment you aren't coming back. Certainly it must be difficult to separate yourself from the places and people that made up your brother's world. I understand you. Lucrezia doesn't understand you. But sometimes Lucrezia can be lacking in sensitivity. She views human feelings in a rough, business-like way.

I am going through a difficult time. I work reluctantly, and everything wears me out. These days I can't bear my partner, Doctor Corsi. It bores me to see people and I prefer to be alone. The best time for me is here in my office when Doctor Corsi and the secretary have gone home, and I see the sunset over the rooftops, through the window, and then the greyness of the dusk, and then darkness. I go home when it has already been dark for a while. I find the children's noise tiresome and I prefer to arrive after supper is over. The noise continues because we have brought the children up badly and they go to bed late, but at least I don't have to put up with the chaos at supper. I eat alone. It's a really terrible time for me. It'll pass. No point in worrying.

Last Saturday Egisto brought your son and two friends over to see us. You never introduced us to your son, and you rarely talked about him. Now, as you know, he lives in the same building as Egisto, on the floor below.

I liked your son, and also his two friends, a girl who is pregnant and a chap with a black moustache. I thought that one of them was the baby's father – either your son or the other one – but Lucrezia said no, and that I had got hold of quite the wrong end of the stick.

The girl upset me because she is so tiny, and she had a lost look about her. She wanted to see the garden and I went out into the garden with her. She told me she is terrified of dying in childbirth and that she doesn't sleep at night. I told her that millions of women give birth every day without dying. Yes, but every now and then there's one who dies. I told her that I had seen Lucrezia give birth five times. I'd always wanted to be present when her children were born. I told her it wasn't anything to be frightened of. We chatted affectionately for a long time. Meanwhile your son and his friend had gone to Pianura with Lucrezia and Ignazio Fegiz, because Serena wanted to be photographed at the Women's Centre, while she was acting a new play in which she is Jocasta – wearing a sheet with a long military cloak over it. Your son and his friend are good photographers, and then Serena had got hold of the notion that they know people in the theatre world and that they could help her break into it. An argument erupted over supper between Serena and Ignazio Fegiz, less of an argument than a real row, about Pirandello whom Serena adores and whom he can't abide. Ignazio Fegiz loses his temper easily, and it seems to me that he has no respect for any one else's opinions. I like Pirandello and I don't find him at all artificial and false as he says, but I'm no expert on the theatre, I rarely go to the theatre. Anyway, I was bored by this argument, and your son and his friends must have been bored to death. Lucrezia was irritable and she finished up arguing with Serena too, not about Pirandello but because Serena had said that the children eat badly and that they are pests.

Your son isn't like you at all. You are both very thin, but his thinness is loose and lazy, whereas yours is angular, straight and lean. I like him, even if he seems a bit strange to me, as young people are these days; you never really know what they think of you, whether they respect you a little or consider you a perfect imbecile. He always seems sleepy and abstracted, but you sense that hidden inside him there is a sharp curiosity about others, and that he conceals his judgements – which are as prickly and sharp as thorns – of other people.

Your son and his friend slept in the room that has the quilts with dragons on them, and the green wardrobe in it; the girl asked if she could sleep with Cecilia because she gets frightened when she sleeps alone in a new place.

Although I don't want to see anyone these days, as I told you, I enjoyed seeing your son here at *Le Margherite*, where you always came without ever bringing him – goodness knows why.

With love from

Piero

20th May

I forgot to post this letter and it's remained here on my table for ten days. Egisto came yesterday. He told us that that girl, Nadia, had her baby without any complications a few days ago. Your son and Egisto took her to the hospital at night, in Egisto's car. She had a girl who is doing well.

IGNAZIO FEGIZ TO GIUSEPPE

Rome, 6th June

Dear Giuseppe,

I am not a letter writer. When your brother died I didn't write you a word. I am sorry about this.

According to Lucrezia I should write to you and tell you to return to Rome. I obey her and write that you should return. All the same, I don't know if you wouldn't be better off staying in America. I don't know. I don't know you at all well. We had hardly made each other's acquaintance when the relationship was almost immediately interrupted. We were divided by the ocean. All the same I often think about you.

I am passing through a rather difficult period. I sleep very little. I get up during the night and walk about the city until morning.

But now I want to tell you that I often see your son, Nadia, and a young man with a big moustache called Salvatore. I saw them one Saturday at *Le Margherite*, then I went and called on them a few times at their flat. The first time I went because they wanted to read me some notes they had jotted down for a film. It is a detective film with an extremely complicated plot and a lot of dead bodies. Nadia has had a baby girl. She came home from the hospital a few days ago. I don't know if you know that your son has registered the child as his daughter. He decided to do this because he likes the baby a lot. He says he will never have children of his own and so he is happy that there should be a baby with his name. Nadia agreed immediately. You could marry me too she said, that would make my parents happy. But he said no, certainly not that. Nadia was chattering away while she gave the baby her breast, and Alberico and Salvatore were shelling beans. It was a very charming little family picture.

I took a friend of mine to their place one day. Her name is Ippolita Teodori. When you came to my house you saw her pictures. She likes new-born babies and she likes people like your son, Nadia and Salvatore. In fact she felt very at ease there. She invited them to have supper on her terrace one evening. She lives in Porta Cavalleggeri. She cooks very well and her terrace is pleasantly cool. They will take the baby because they have bought one of those portable things you put babies in. They have also bought a car, a Panda. It doesn't seem to me that they have any problems about money. I wanted to give you all this news because it seems to be good news to me.

Yours affectionately

Ignazio

GIUSEPPE TO IGNAZIO FEGIZ

Princeton, 20th June

Dear Ignazio,

Thank you for your letter.

I'm glad that you see my son. The news you give me about him is very reassuring. My cousin Roberta phoned me a few days ago and I knew from her that Alberico has registered the baby as his. The baby is called Giorgia, like my mother. Her surname is Guaraldi, like mine. In a way I've become a grandfather.

I'm glad that you often go to *Le Margherite*. And I'm generally glad to think of you involved in my former life. I'm also perhaps a little jealous of you, when I think of you in the places where I am not. But it's a faint jealousy, a vague uneasiness which I feel forming for a few moments and which I then rapidly forget. It's a faint jealousy, with no nails or claws to it.

I haven't much to tell you about myself. Perhaps I'll return to Italy, later, I don't know when. At the moment I don't want to decide. I've lost my brother and I think of myself, for the moment, as being exempt from making decisions. At the moment it would be painful to detach myself from the life I have established here. I'm writing a novel. I go cycling. I teach. I am a bit of company for Anne Marie, my brother's widow. She is a person I get on well with, even though we have nothing to talk to each other about. She is only interested in scientific research, but scientific subjects are all Greek to me. And so we talk very little. Sometimes, very rarely, we talk about my brother.

Yours affectionately

Giuseppe

ALBERICO TO GIUSEPPE

Rome, 23rd June

Respected father,

As perhaps you've heard, I've given my name to a child. I thought I ought to tell you as my name is also yours. The baby's mother is Nadia, that girl you saw with me in Florence. She is a very stupid girl, but I like her well enough. I live with her. I like the baby, she's very pretty. I want to be her father, not just in name, but in fact as well. I want to give her what I never had, a father's protection. You were never very present in my life. You weren't much of a father. Not that it matters, it's water under the bridge now. If you come to Rome I'll introduce you to my baby girl.

Alberico

GIUSEPPE TO ALBERICO

Princeton, 30th June

Respected son,

I had heard about the baby. I think what you've done is a good thing. The notion of having a baby daughter, whether or not she's actually yours, will give you a desire for stability. However, you then have to find ways of turning this desire into a reality. Last month you were twenty-six. You could do with a permanent job, but you haven't got one. You jump from one job to another. It's true that you have money, but that will come to an end one day. As you know already, I've no money to leave you; you are, as you know, richer than I am. You will have to support the baby.

Perhaps you thought that saying I wasn't much of a father would hurt me. But you haven't hurt me. I know well enough that as a father I've given you very little. I hope that you will be a better father than I was.

And so in a sense I've become a grandfather. Strange. I feel very young still, but clearly I'm not. But it's not entirely true that I feel young. Sometimes I feel that I'm an old man with an immense past behind me.

If you come to Princeton you can meet Anne Marie. I get on well with her. The memory of my brother, who loved her, is a bond between us. We don't talk much. We don't spend much time together. She has started her work at the Institute – which she had given up temporarily – again. I stay in my room and write. However, we go for walks together sometimes, or we sit in the drawing-room, she knits and I sit and watch her and every now and then say something to her. I think she's very intelligent, but I can't appreciate anything of her intelligence because we have nothing in common and the things that interest her don't interest me at all. It doesn't matter, we keep each other company anyway.

Anne Marie has a daughter who lives in Philadelphia and who is called Chantal. Two months ago Chantal had a baby girl. We went to see her a few weeks ago. Chantal isn't happy with her husband. I think their marriage is on the point of breaking up. The baby is very pretty. And so there are these baby girls in our lives now.

With love from

your father

EGISTO TO GIUSEPPE

Rome, 1st July

Dear Giuseppe,

I have never written to you and I feel very guilty about this. Your brother died and I neither wrote to you nor phoned. I could have phoned you from the newspaper without spending a single lira, but I didn't do it. Sad things that happen to other people make me feel diffident.

I'll tell you about your son, whom I see virtually every day. We usually meet on the stairs with the rubbish bags. Sometimes he is carrying the baby. He is a loving father to that child. He often takes her to the park in her pram. It's a very splendid pram. They have borrowed it. They keep it at the bottom of the stairs. Sometimes your son's friend Salvatore goes to the park with the pram. He wears a red sweatshirt and has a big black moustache. They both seem very sweet with the baby, and I like this side of them. The baby's mother, Nadia, sleeps a lot and doesn't go out much. Every now and then the three of them have violent rows and they all yell simultaneously – I hear the yelling and go out on the balcony, but I think the rows are usually about stupid, trivial things, the words I catch are about clothes that have to be hung out to dry or potatoes that have to be peeled. When they first moved in Nadia used to come up and ask me if she could use my washing-machine, but she doesn't any more because they've bought one.

The other day Nadia's parents came up from Sicily. The father is a little old man with a small bristly grey beard. The mother is a tired, elegant old woman. A huge row suddenly broke out, I think between Nadia and her parents. Salvatore came up and asked me for some lemons. The row died down and from my balcony I saw them having tea and biscuits. Your cousin Roberta was there too. The two old folks, Roberta later told me, left after a few days with the idea that your son Alberico was the baby's real father, and in the firm belief that the whole thing was a disaster. They didn't even like Roberta and were very frosty to her.

I tell you these things because they concern your son and I think that they will interest you. Even though I don't go down that often I see them on the stairs and from my balcony. I don't go down that often because, to be honest with you, I don't feel completely at ease with them. They are more or less my age but I feel myself to be much older than them. They intrigue me, but they make me feel diffident, which is a peculiar sensation.

I took them to *Le Margherite*. They made no comment on either Piero or Lucrezia, nor on Albina or Serena. I don't know whether they enjoyed themselves or were bored. Nadia said only that her mattress was lumpy. Which was probably true. I've finished up with terrible mattresses at *Le Margherite*.

They often have friends round. I see people in their house from my balcony. I envy them because I'm pretty much alone. I sometimes go to the Rotunnos', or to one of my colleague's at the newspaper, but I hold back from phoning too much, I'm afraid of seeming pushy. I'm basically very diffident, and there are few people I get on well with.

Getting back to your son, I know that one evening they went to supper at Ippolita's, that girl-friend of Ignazio Fegiz who lives in Porta Cavalleggeri. Afterwards this Ippolita woman came to see them quite often, and I saw her sitting on a deck-chair – their balcony is right under mine. She is a slim, elegant woman with a big hooked nose and a thick mane of golden hair. Ignazio Fegiz has been with her for a very long time. But they don't live together.

Albina is well. We sometimes eat together in the evenings, sometimes at Mariuccia's where we always used to go with you and where even the walls remind us of you. To tell you the truth I'm a bit bored with her, we always say the same things, we always talk about the same people. Being with her is a bit like being alone for me. But she is a good person, she is fond of me and I'm fond of her too. When she asks me to have supper with her I don't know how to say no. Perhaps she wants to go to bed with me, I don't know, in any case she doesn't attract me at all physically. I think she claims that it's me who's after her, and that she doesn't want me. She's lying, because I've always let her know that I'm attracted by a quite different kind of woman.

I don't have very much that's new to tell you about our friends at Monte Fermo and Pianura – I mean Piero and Lucrezia and Serena. Everything is more or less as it was when you left. The Woman's Centre goes laboriously forward, there's never much on there and not many people go. Serena is pleased with it but she will close it down soon because she's going on a trip to Russia. Piero and Lucrezia will stay at Monte Fermo even during August. This is not at all how things normally are, because they used to take the children to the seaside, but they say they don't want to this year. Every morning the children go off with the Swiss au pair to play in the stream. As this Swiss girl is extremely stupid I'm always afraid she'll let one of them drown. Lucrezia says she is stupid but sensible. Nevertheless she sunbathes stretched out on a rock with her eyes closed. She could at least lie there with her eyes open. I don't know whether Piero and Lucrezia perhaps have some problem about money. He seems depressed and she seems irritable. But then it's happened before that they have been depressed and irritable. I don't think that there are serious difficulties – either economic or matrimonial – between them. But certainly at the moment, what with her being so irritable and him being so gloomy they are not very pleasant company and you always have the feeling you are bothering them, so I go there less willingly.

You are always in my thoughts.

Yours

Egisto

LUCREZIA TO GIUSEPPE

Monte Fermo, 20th July

Dear Giuseppe,

All of a sudden I've a great desire to write to you. So I've locked the door to my room so that no one can come and annoy me while I'm writing to you.

It's five in the afternoon and it's very hot. Everyone's in a bad mood, perhaps because of the heat. A short while ago there was a great row between my mother-in law and the Swiss girl, because my mother-in-law went into the Swiss girl's room and the bed had not been made yet and she saw that the mattress was stained with menstrual blood. Then she saw biscuit-crumbs and ants under the bed.

This row irritated me. I found both of them unbearable. The Swiss girl said she would leave tomorrow and took her suitcases down from the top of the wardrobe. I tried to calm her down but without success. If she leaves tomorrow I shall have everything to manage – the children and the house at a time when I want to just stay quietly in my room and think.

So many things have happened to me since you left. My life has changed. I've fallen in love. You will be surprised if I tell you that I've never been in love before, when I always kept telling you that I fall in love very easily, but they were all mistakes, and perhaps you'll be offended if I tell you that you were a mistake too. I thought I was in love with you, I thought I wanted to live with you – what a mistake, Giuseppe – you, thank goodness, were terrified at the prospect and told me for God's sake to stay where I was. You were wise and I thank you for it. I got on with you well enough, at the beginning, I felt happy enough, but it was all on the level of enough. When I met you my life did not change colour. Now it has changed colour. Piero accepted you, he stayed calm, more or less, my adultery with you was a bloodless affair. Now, on the contrary, my adultery is of the kind that scatters blood all over the place. I.F. and I are madly in love with each other and we are going to live together, I don't know when. I don't know where. We shall get a house in a town, I don't know which one. I shall take the children with me. You were afraid of the children, he isn't, he isn't afraid of anything.

When I saw him arrive here the first time and get out of his olive-green Renault and come towards me with that grey crew-cut he has, I suddenly felt scared and irritated. I said to myself 'Now who in God's name can this be?' We paused for a moment and looked at each other, not moving, face to face. We are about the same height – I'm a very little taller than he is, but only a very little. The dogs started barking. They didn't want him there. Egisto and Albina were behind him and they were surprised that the dogs were barking, usually they don't bark. From that moment I have liked Egisto and Albina even more and I really enjoy seeing them. He went into the house and hung his raincoat on the coat-stand and immediately a nail came out of the wall and the coat-stand came crashing down. Goodness knows why a nail should come out of the wall at that precise moment. Afterwards I told him that the dogs barking and the coat-stand coming down had been two omens.

I think that Piero quickly realized that something was going on because his manner changed immediately, from the first few times that I.F. started coming here on Saturdays he seemed as if always frightened and upset. At first he only came on Saturday, but then on other days during the week too. He would 'phone and then come over. Now he doesn't come any more. Sometimes we meet in Pianura and go for a walk in the country. But usually I go to his house in Rome. He has that relationship with that woman called Ippolita, though everyone calls her Ippo. They don't live together. She's a woman with a big nose and beautiful hair. Everybody tells me about her hair. Everybody – Albina, Egisto – tells me about it. What on earth's so marvellous about her hair! I've never seen her. Egisto's seen her, he's been in her house. She has a very beautiful terrace. Everybody talks about her terrace too. I.F. finds it difficult to leave her because it will hurt her, he hasn't told her anything about me, but in a few days now he's going to tell her about me and leave her. It hasn't been easy for me to talk to Piero either, but I had to talk to him because I would have felt bad if I hadn't talked to him. Anyway, Piero had already realized everything. He's very depressed. We had an open relationship – you remember that we were always saying so – but in fact it was only open on my side, Piero has never loved any other woman than me. Anyway an open relationship reaches a point when it either closes or goes to pieces. The relationship between Piero and me is going to pieces. I'm sorry because I'm fond of Piero, I'm sorry to see him depressed. I feel that he wouldn't have been so depressed if I had gone off with you, but he thinks of I.F. as something dreadful. He always comes home very late from Perugia and eats alone; I sit myself down at the table whilst he's eating and he tells me to go away. He can't stand me and I can't stand him. We sleep together but on some nights I tell him I'm too hot and I go and sleep upstairs in the room that has the quilts with dragons on them . It should be cooler in there because it faces west, but in fact it's stiflingly hot in there too. Sometimes I'm very unhappy as well.

The strange thing is that everything is breaking up here, the whole house is falling to pieces. The Swiss girl is leaving tomorrow, the washing-machine leaks. It's very hot, we're all dead with the heat. The Swiss girl used to take the children to the stream every day, but she's going tomorrow and I shall have to take them because if I don't they will wander round the garden getting bored and filthy. Serena has gone to Russia, otherwise she could have taken them to the stream. I think the children have realized something is going on too, because they all seem frightened and bored. Perhaps the Swiss girl has realized too and that's why she's going, because it isn't very cheerful staying somewhere where everything's falling to pieces. Only my mother-in-law hasn't realized anything. Every so often she comes to me with a worried look on her face and tells me that she has found a dead bird full of ants on the bathroom window-sill, or she tells me she's found a bowl of mouldy figs in the refrigerator. Whenever my mother-in-law goes round the house these days she always find something disgusting.

You are really my only friend. And so I'm very very sorry that you're so far away just at the time when I need to confide in someone. Serena isn't here now either. But then I'm not so sure that Serena would listen to me and understand. I think she would immediately take Piero's side. Her head's always full of the position of women, women's rights. etc., but I know only too well that she would despise me. Sometimes I talk to Albina when she comes on Saturdays. I tell her something, not everything, of how things stand. But my one real friend is you. And you have to go and hole yourself up in America. Our long affair has left us with a deep friendship for each other. I feel it for you and I hope you feel it for me. We've also had a son together, Graziano. You don't want me to say so but it's true. A son together and a deep friendship. These are the good things I have given to you and which you have given to me, the good things that we own together. You don't give a damn about your son and you pretend he's nothing to do with you – as you wish, it doesn't matter. But I think you will acknowledge our friendship as real.

Your son Alberico came here once. But afterwards so many things happened that I forgot to tell you about it. I don't know if I like this son of yours. I don't understand him very well. He gave his name to that girl's baby. Of course he did it to be the opposite of you, to be what you don't want to be, the father of a child coming into the world.

Send me your news. And tell me what's happening to you. Let me know if you're still sleeping in the room with the bear-cubs.

Lucrezia

GIUSEPPE TO LUCREZIA

Princeton, 4th August

Dear Lucrezia,

Your letter moved me a great deal, so much so that I couldn't work for the whole day. You know I'm writing a novel, I think I've mentioned it to you. Your letter got so tangled up with my thoughts that I couldn't free myself from it, and I found your face and your voice everywhere inside me. I didn't answer immediately. I let a few days pass, because it upset me to answer you.

You are in love with Ignazio Fegiz, or with I.F. as you call him. This should not mean anything to me, or rather it should please me, because falling in love is a splendid thing and because a person is pleased if something splendid happens to someone he is fond of. Instead, I felt uneasy as I read your letter. You want to leave Piero and go and live with I.F. and take your children with you. You tend to think of your children as if they were furniture or luggage. Besides, there are five of them, not just one. If there was one you could put everything into reassuring him. But it's not easy to reassure five children. And for I.F. too, five children is not going to be a small undertaking. You say that 'he's not afraid of anything'. As for yourself I have to tell you that at the very least I think you are being reckless. And I have to think the same about him.

What you say about us, about you and me, 'our adultery was a bloodless affair' seems ridiculous to me. No adultery is bloodless. And then according to you we have had a son together. I don't think that's true, but if it is true our adultery was not a bloodless affair. Children are blood, and they are born surrounded by blood.

I felt there was something lurking behind your whole letter, something that hurt me deeply, an obscure desire to compare I.F. and me with each other, and to see me as someone inferior, less noble, less valued. Your dogs barked for him. The coat-stand fell down for him. Then you say that he is about the same height as you. You know very well that I hardly come up to your shoulders, and that this always upset me.

You say 'I got on with you well enough, I felt happy enough, it was all on the level of enough'. How nasty you can be. How cruel. You know how to make someone suffer. I don't believe that you don't know.

As for your dithyrambs about our friendship, I have to tell you that I find them hard to believe, and so I don't know how to respond to them. Real friendship does not scratch and bite, and your letter scratched and bit me.

What shall I tell you about myself. I get along well. Well enough. On the level of enough, of course. I'm content. The school is closed at the moment. I'm on holiday. I start again in September. I'm writing my novel. Anne Marie gets back from the Institute around six in the evening. I watch her while she's making the dinner, a complicated dinner, big rissoles that have to be cooked slowly, with carrots and stock, soups made with beetroot and cream, Russian dishes that I've learnt to love. Anne Marie had a Russian grandmother. We say very little. Anne Marie is someone who says very little, and always in a low voice, and I like that. I find it restful to live with someone who weighs her words, who speaks sparingly and judiciously. Anne Marie smiles all the time and I have learnt to smile all the time too whilst she is there. Sometimes my mouth is a little tired with the effort of all that smiling. But I think that little by little we shall finally stop smiling.

No, I don't sleep in the room with the bear-cubs. I sleep upstairs. But I don't sleep with Anne Marie, if that's what you want to know.

Giuseppe

ALBINA TO EGISTO

Luco dei Marsi, 3rd August

Dear Egisto,

As you see I am with my family again. I have to stay in Luco for a fortnight. My mother hasn't got up yet and the relative who was helping her has gone away and won't come back till after mid-August, after the Feast of the Assumption. And so my holidays have vanished. On top of which I made a huge mistake in bringing Vito here with me. He's the worst of Lucrezia's children, the biggest pest, even though he's only little. Lucrezia insisted I bring him with me. The Swiss girl packed her bags one fine morning and left. She's never going to show herself there again. Lucrezia is tired. On top of which relations between her and Piero get worse and worse. There is an unbearable atmosphere in that house now. It's a desolate atmosphere. They've sent Cecilia to Montecatini with Piero's mother, Signora Annina. Signora Annina hasn't understood a thing though she and Lucrezia argue about ridiculous things like telephone bills and rotten tomatoes. And so it was a relief for everyone when she said she wanted to go to Montecatini. They have sent Daniele, Augusto and Graziano off to a summer camp. So that now there is just Piero and Lucrezia at *Le Margherite*, face to face in the heat and the silence. When I was there I talked a little first with one then with the other; I tried to calm them down and make peace. But I was half dead by the end of the day because at the moment they are both being unbearably difficult, people really are exhausting when they talk reams of nonsense and don't know what to do. And to be plain Lucrezia has had affairs before, she had a very long affair with Giuseppe, and other shorter ones, but they were just child's play she says. Piero stayed calm. He pretended not to care. She and Piero had an open relationship. They were always saying so. They stayed friends. But now they are not friends any more and Piero is fed up. And Lucrezia is fed up too, though she says she is happier than she has ever been before, she says she is happy and unhappy all together. Every so often she jumps into the Volkswagen and goes off to Rome. She returns the next day. She says that she will leave before autumn. She will live with Ignazio Fegiz, I don't know where, even she doesn't know. And certainly Ignazio Fegiz doesn't know. Not, I think, in Rome. Perhaps in America. Lucrezia will take all her children with her. She says she won't leave the children. This is the only thing she feels certain about. But Piero doesn't want to let her have the children. I don't know what they're going to do.

They will need a lot of money to move everyone to America. Lucrezia says that I.F. – she always refers to him like that, as I.F. – has plenty of money because he is a picture-dealer, and that she will find herself a job. However she has never done anything in her life and she doesn't have any idea what kind of work she could do. She is vague on the subject of work. She wrinkles her forehead and waves her fingers about in the air.

I don't like I.F. I don't trust him at all. He seems to me to be someone with a weak character pretending he has a strong character. I told Lucrezia that. She told me I hadn't understood anything, as usual. She feels protected and secure. When she feels unhappy she is unhappy because now she finds herself carrying around the weight of so many ruined years.

Egisto, you and I won't be able to go to *Le Margherite* on Saturdays next winter. We shall never go there again, it's finished. This really saddens me. Piero says he will sell *Le Margherite* as soon as possible. He will move to Perugia with the children. Lucrezia says that on the contrary she and the children will be in America in a few months, or perhaps in Paris, or in Belgium where she has an uncle.

Because someone has to be with Vito from morning till night Lucrezia begged me to take him away with me. She said that it's cool at Luco dei Marsi and that he'd be better off there than in Monte Fermo. I couldn't refuse her. But as soon as I got on the train with Vito I realized I'd made a huge mistake. Vito is a sweet child but he is a real pest. I shan't ever forget that train journey. He went backwards and forwards along the corridor; the train was crowded and the corridor was full of luggage and people. I had to follow him and I was afraid that someone would take my seat in the meantime. I bought him an ice cream and he left smears of ice-cream everywhere. Lucrezia is very tired, but then I'm tired too. I hoped that here in my house Maura and Gina would look after Vito but they wouldn't hear of it. I don't know, there was a time when young girls were pleased to take little children out for walks, but it's not like that any more. As soon as I suggested that Maura and Gina take Vito out they disappeared like hares. Never mind, it was a mistake and we have to pay for our mistakes. Vito wants to be with my mother all the time, he's crazy about my mother, he wants to scribble with his crayons all over her leg that's in plaster. My mother is patient with him for a while but then she gets annoyed and asks me what the devil I thought I was doing turning up with this child. Vito has two obsessions, one is to climb up on to the window-sills and the other is to go into the kitchen and turn all the gas taps on. So I live in terror. I've promised to keep him here till mid August.

Love

Albina

EGISTO TO ALBINA

Rome, 10th August

Dear Albina,

I shall leave in two days' time for my holiday. I've booked a room in a pensione in Follonica. It is incredibly hot in Rome. I take a shower every half hour.

I know everything you told me about Piero and Lucrezia. I was at *Le Margherite* two days after you left. I had to put up with all their tirades too. They were silent up to a month ago, but now they talk non-stop, every moment one of them drags you into a room and wants you to sit down and listen.

I don't believe that Lucrezia really wants to leave Piero. I don't believe that she wants to go and live in Paris or America or goodness knows where. She says it just to have something to say. I don't believe in this great love of hers. She's going through a time of crisis, as happens to women around forty. Because Lucrezia must be forty by now.

I had dinner one evening with Ignazio Fegiz and his friend Ippo. I met them by chance in Piazza di Spagna. I saw them coming towards me, she was dressed in black and looked rather frail, and he looked sturdy in a crumpled white suit. I don't know why but it seemed to me I was seeing the Cat and the Fox. I went for dinner with them, to Augusteo's. She is a strange woman. She is ugly but she has beautiful hair. She parts it in the middle, and out of her hair appears a long, hooked nose – she is all hair and nose. At the restaurant we ordered macaroni-cheese and meat, she ordered grated carrots, a cup of vegetable broth and that was it. She was afraid the broth might have been made with a bouillon cube and so she sniffed at it for a long time with her long nose.

Ippo dresses well. She had on a skirt made of black satin, a kind of long, tight tube, and a starched white blouse with a little cravat. No trinkets. An onyx ring on one finger. People say she takes drugs, I don't know. Ignazio Fegiz becomes different when she is there. He's usually aggressive and noisy and doesn't let anyone talk, and instead he's silent when she is there. He looks at her. It's as if there is a continuous and very old understanding between them. We went to her place after supper. She lives in Porta Cavalleggeri. Her flat is really tiny and completely full of pictures. They are almost all her pictures. They are landscapes. They are a reddish, gold colour as if she's always thinking about sunsets, and after a while all that reddish-gold tires your eyes. The terrace is cool. We drank iced wine and stayed there talking for a long time. To tell the truth she did the talking by herself. She has travelled the world, she has been to China and Japan. I looked at her and thought that next to her our Lucrezia wouldn't seem much to write home about. She would seem too tall, her feet and hands would be too big, she'd be badly dressed and wouldn't have a single trip abroad to talk about. We stayed there till it was late. Before he left Ignazio watered the plants. I got the impression that he does this every evening.

Ignazio Fegiz left with me. As soon as we were in the street he was his old self again, noisy, talkative, nothing at all cat-like about him. Neither he nor I had a car. The nights are cool and it's pleasant to walk through the city. He likes the summer. But it also seems a malevolent season to him because lots of people go mad during the summer. He didn't once mention Lucrezia. I told him that I had been to *Le Margherite*. He said that unlike me he hadn't been there for a while.

I think that Lucrezia has imagined this great love. As far as I can see Ignazio Fegiz is someone who doesn't want to change his private life one iota.

How you go on about Vito, the poor child. He's irritating, certainly. All children are irritating. But don't go on about him so much. If you didn't want him in the house you should have thought of that before.

My neighbours haven't left. Yesterday I went down to get the pressure-cooker I'd lent them. They never return things. A girl in a violet-coloured bikini opened the door to me, she was very thin with a mane of carroty hair. Though it's true that I see carrots everywhere these days ever since I saw Ippo eating them.

Nadia was in the kitchen – also in a bikini – she was mixing a rice salad; she had that sullen, gloomy look she always has. The girl in the bikini is an American and she is called Anais. I mentioned the writer Anais Nin but they had never heard of her. There was an incredible mess in the kitchen. They had had people around the previous evening. I helped Nadia to cut up some zucchini. The baby was crying. They had put her on the balcony in a baby-chair, under an umbrella, but the sun was on her legs and she was covered in sweat. I suggested they bring her in and give her something to drink. They brought her in and stuck a feeding-bottle full of orange juice in her mouth. These modern girls don't know how to look after a baby. Then Alberico and Salvatore appeared from one of the rooms in their vests and underpants, still very sleepy and dishevelled. They looked like a couple of owls. Alberico got angry because the plates had not been washed yet. I ate with them. First the rice salad then an omelette I made. Then Salvatore and I washed the plates. The baby cried the whole time.

Yours

Egisto

PIERO TO GIUSEPPE

Monte Fermo, 25th August

Dear Giuseppe,

I haven't had any reply to a letter I wrote you about two months ago. Perhaps you didn't receive it, or perhaps you didn't think it necessary to answer me. The latter seems more likely to me. At the moment I tend to think no one can be bothered with me.

Lucrezia has gone. I don't know where she's gone, she didn't tell me. I'm alone in this house which I loved so much, and which I now hate. My mother and children are away. I don't know where Lucrezia is. It's terrible to think about someone all the time and not know where she is. She just jumped into her Volkswagen one morning. I saw her swimming flippers sticking out of her bag. I asked her where she was going and she said she didn't know. She said she would phone me. I asked her if she had enough money and she said she had. It's been eight days now and she hasn't phoned yet.

I get in my car every morning and go to Perugia. I haven't got anything to do at the office but I go there just the same. At least it's air-conditioned there. Doctor Corsi is on holiday and so are both our secretaries. I eat in a little café nearby. This is what my life is going to be like when Lucrezia has gone for good.

She told me she would take the children with her. I told her I would never allow her to. This isn't true, I know very well that she will do whatever she's decided on. She has a strong character. I'm a weak person. I've trailed this feeling of being weak around with me since I was a child. She will give me the children one day a week and for a month in the summer. It happens like this for lots of people, lots of men. Normally when a marriage goes to pieces the women take the children. In the summer the children will be with me. I won't know what to say to them, because you don't know what to say to children when they're with you for one month a year. There are too many things you want to tell them, and they stick in your throat. I think that during that month one would try and be as kind and easy-going as possible so that they will love you and have good memories of you throughout the winter. I think that this effort to be kind and easy-going with your own children must be very exhausting. And it must be something that makes you feel contemptible. And then it's a mistake because children don't like an easy-going atmosphere. They like to have strict, authoritative people around them. People suspect it's a mistake, but they do it anyway. That's what I shall do too.

You had a long relationship lasting several years with Lucrezia. This will seem strange to you, but it never upset me. I stayed calm. I knew that we weren't going to be hurt by it. You're not someone who hurts people, you are someone who is careful not to hurt people as he goes by, not to trample on or destroy anything. You and I are birds of a feather. You are one of those who always loses.

I realize that I've written without giving you any explanation, as if you already knew everything. But I imagine that Lucrezia has already told you. We have decided to separate. Or rather, she has decided. I haven't decided anything. I bowed my head and accepted.

My mother will come back in a few days. She and I will be alone. The children are all at Forte dei Marmi at the moment, with my sister. My mother doesn't know anything. I shall have to tell her and I dread it. She will cry, she'll be full of pity for me and it's very difficult to put up with pity from one's parents. It's much easier to put up with pity from one's children. Goodness knows why.

My mother will cry. I shall have to comfort her. I shall have to tell her that I'm all right. Reasonably all right. I shall have to tell her that these things often happen.

I'm always thinking of you.

Yours

Piero

GIUSEPPE TO PIERO

Princeton, 30th August

Dear Piero,

I had heard what you wrote to me from Lucrezia.

I did get your other letter. I didn't reply not because I didn't think it necessary to answer you, but because I found it difficult to do so, as I had sensed from a distance things that you didn't mention, and as I had had letters from Lucrezia that said everything.

Even now it's not easy for me to write to you and tell you what I went through as I read your last letter. It isn't easy to tell you how close I feel to you in this disaster that's overtaken you. I think of it as a disaster for both of you, even though only you are suffering at the moment, and she perhaps is happy, or thinks she is.

I'm sorry not to be with you at Monte Fermo, not to go for walks with you in the woods and over the little hills there as we have done so many times. You know that you have a loyal friend in me, even though in the past I betrayed you – though we stayed friends – in the way you know about. It's not that I'm someone who is careful not to hurt anyone as he goes by, not to trample on or destroy things. It's not true. I have destroyed and trampled underfoot a great many things that were in my way. In fact when I get up in the morning I find in myself a deep disgust for what I am, for my feet in their slippers, for my sad face in the mirror, for my clothes draped over the chair. As the day goes on this disgust becomes gradually more and more stifling.

As you know I'm not returning to Italy for the moment. I'm writing a novel and I want to finish it. Besides, I have a relationship here with someone, a strange relationship that's quite different from all the others I've previously had with women.

It's a woman I'm talking about. It's Anne Marie, my brother's widow. My brother was very fond of her and for this reason I am very fond of her. But she and I don't talk to each other, or we say very little. It's a relationship of smiles and murmurs. It's a relationship that seems calm, but inwardly it is shaken by continual shocks.

I too am always thinking of you.

Yours

Giuseppe

EGISTO TO ALBINA

Rome, 27th August

Dear Albina,

I stayed in Follonica for a week. Just imagine, I'd been there for two days when I saw my neighbours from downstairs arriving. I was in the little garden of my pensione reading the newspapers when I saw them getting out of their little maroon Panda. I'd told them in passing where I was going, and they came. It's strange, sometimes I don't go down to them because I'm afraid of bothering them, and then they follow me to Follonica. Strange. You name them a place and immediately they come after you. They had rucksacks and blankets and they put the baby in a little rucksack affair which they took in turns to hoist on to their backs, to carry her around. They had a tent for sleeping on the beach, which they did, all except for Nadia and the baby who slept in my pensione; however there weren't any rooms free and so I had to give her mine. I slept in a bathroom. I don't like sleeping in bathrooms at all, I like rooms with beds in them, but I couldn't do anything else – I realized that the baby was too little to sleep in a tent. There was a sudden downpour one night and Salvatore came to the pensione to find me. I hadn't gone to bed yet. The tent had collapsed in the wind and they wanted me to help them put it up again. We re-erected the tent in the pouring rain. I was drenched to the skin. And then their mattresses were completely soaked and they bundled themselves into the Panda to sleep.

I don't know if they feel any affection for me. Perhaps they do, seeing that they came to Follonica where I was staying. But perhaps that was just lack of imagination. I don't know if I feel any affection for them. They intrigue me, and then as you know I'm alone a lot. We don't have anything to talk about. If we talked about the big subjects – politics or whatever – I don't think we would agree about anything. At Follonica I tried to find neutral, inoffensive subjects. The tent. The baby. The film. That film they say they are making. But they let every subject drop. Occasionally violent arguments broke out between them. They were ridiculous arguments about a tent-peg or a camping-stool, but they yelled like wild animals and seemed on the point of tearing each other limb from limb. I don't know if they take drugs. I suspect it, but I'm not sure. They smoke joints. I've smoked them occasionally when I've been with them, out of politeness and not to seem old-fashioned but I prefer *Marlboros*. They had bought a plastic basin in the country which they used to fill with sea-water; they'd let it warm up in the sun and then bath the baby. But that baby is very tiny, she's only three months old, and I was always afraid that they would harm her with all the heat and the sea-water and the feeding bottles of orange juice which they left for ages in the sun and let them get filthy in the sand and then stuck in her mouth. Nadia is one of those people who is terrified of everything, for herself; a wasp stung her and Alberico had to rush off and find some ammonia. Alberico was cursing but he quickly came back with ammonia, cotton wool and little packets of sterile gauze. For the baby on the other hand Nadia never fears anything. It never occurs to her that anything could hurt the baby. Her milk has dried up and she gives her baby-food which she buys, mixtures of flour and goodness knows what else; she goes into a bar and asks for a little hot water, tips the lot into a bottle and she's away. Then Alberico washes the bottle at a public fountain. She doesn't remember to and she'd be quite happy to use it still filthy.

Anais intrigues me the most of all. She is not beautiful but I find her quite pretty. She and I have made love three times. Once in the bathroom of the pensione, where I had my bed. Once behind some bushes. Once here in Rome in my house, about an hour ago. She is going back to America in two weeks time. That doesn't mean much to me. In fact it means virtually nothing to me. I haven't been able to find out much about her. She speaks Italian badly and I speak English badly. She has an eight-year-old son in America. Her mother looks after him. The boy's father was a Pakistani. She is a millionaire. She didn't tell me that, the others told me.

We came back to Rome two days ago. Anais is sleeping at the other side of my room. She says that no one bothers her when she is here in my flat, but down below there's all hell going on – the baby crying, and yelling about one thing and another. Yesterday Salvatore slapped Nadia and made her nose bleed. I think she'd called him a fucking queen, or something like that. I arrived when it had already happened. Nadia was lying on the bed with a wad of something to stop the bleeding, Salvatore was cooking a chicken stew, Alberico was typing. When Alberico saw me come in he looked pleased. He made me a coffee and told me about his film. He had already told me a little about it during the journey from Follonica to Rome. He and Anais travelled in my car. To be more comfortable, they said, and also to keep me company. I thought that was kind of them. The film is extremely complicated and full of corpses.

Come away from Luco soon, come back to Rome. I'll take you out to dinner. You'll meet Anais.

Egisto

ROBERTA TO GIUSEPPE

Rome, 22nd September

Dear Giuseppe,

We haven't written to each other for a while now. For months we've just talked over the phone and that's been it. But when you're making international telephone calls you think about the money you're spending and so you finish up not saying anything. So many more things can be said in a letter.

As I told you on the phone, Alberico has agreed to undergo psychoanalysis, after I had strenuously insisted that he should. He comes and sees Doctor Lanzara four times a week, at two in the afternoon. He started on the 10th September. He's been punctual so far. I asked Lanzara if the fact that his consulting room is in what was once your flat might disturb Alberico and remind him too much of you. Lanzara thought about it for a while but then he said it wasn't important. Besides the flat is completely different now, it seems virtually unrecognizable.

After each session Alberico comes down to my flat and has a coffee. In this way I see him often, which pleases me. He seems fairly well to me. As ever he's very thin and pale, and has that shuffling way of walking; he wears sandals and his feet are always filthy. He always seems like somebody who has just walked for miles and miles. Though in reality he's just caught the bus in Piazza Sonnino and got out a few yards away from here.

He's working, he says. He's writing the screen-play for a film. He told me the story. I didn't understand any of it.

The film's title is *Deviance*.

I always ask him what he's eaten, because he looks undernourished. However it seems that they eat an incredible amount at his house. They do nothing but cook. Fish, peppers.

The baby has been weaned and is growing well. That's what

he told me. I haven't been to their place for a while. I don't want to bother them. I belong to a different generation.

You will have heard that Piero and Lucrezia are separating. What a pity. I'm very sorry; I remember them together and I can't imagine them apart. She is trying to find a flat in Rome, with the money she inherited from her mother. She has seen a great many but she doesn't like any of them. She has asked me to help her. You know I have a friend who runs an estate agency. Lucrezia wants to have a house in old Rome. But she has very little money. It's not an easy matter by any means.

They are going to sell *Le Margherite*. What a pity. With the money they get from the sale he will buy an apartment in Perugia and the rest will go to her.

How quickly everything is happening. It seems only yesterday that you and I went to *Le Margherite*, that I saw *Le Margherite* in front of me – the porch, the swing, all those children and all those dogs, and that entrance hall where there was a coat-stand that was always overloaded.

I feel sorry for Piero. People tell me he's a broken man. Egisto told me – I met him in a café with a girl who had red hair, an American who was staying with Alberico and the others. Lucrezia is taking all the children with her. She's become Ignazio Fegiz's lover. They're going to live together.

It's unbelievable how quickly everything happens. Goodness only knows what they're going to do with all those dogs. I love dogs and I can't not think about them. It's true though that the main worry is all those children being moved into a flat in the city, and with another father.

I remember that day when Ignazio Fegiz came to your place and then we all came down to mine and made spaghetti. Then I remember that time he took us to Florence in his car. I didn't like him. He was always telling me I was wrong. He's one of those people who always tells everyone they're wrong.

That time we went to Florence was shortly before you left for America. I remember that trip to Florence very well. I remember the last weeks before you left very well. You were very restless. You looked bewildered, wandering about the house, in the midst of all that chaos. Once or twice your brother phoned. He wanted to be sure that you were coming. I can still hear his voice in my ears, curt, deep, authoritative. I congratulated him on his marriage. Goodness, how quickly everything happens.

I didn't really understand what kind of woman Anne Marie is. She was very kind to me, for the few days I was a guest in her house.

I really know nothing about you now. You say so little on the phone.

With love from

Roberta

LUCREZIA TO GIUSEPPE

Rome, 10th October

Dear Giuseppe,

I've been in Rome for a week. I'm here in Roberta's house as she has kindly put me up. I must buy a flat but flats are so dear and I haven't much money. I have the money I inherited from my mother but it's not enough. I've seen some flats but they were small and ugly. I.F. is in Paris and he'll come back around the middle of the month. Besides I've realized that he isn't going to help me find a flat and that I have to look at them myself. I've enrolled the children in schools here. The two eldest will go to the Tasso school, the two little ones to the German school in via Saleria. I have to find a nursery for Vito. I do nothing but go round and round Rome like a spinning top and I'm worn out.

I've just heard from a friend of Serena that she has a flat she could lend me for a year. She's an Australian and she's going back to Australia for a year. The flat is in Piazza del Paradiso. It's a bit dark and there's no central-heating. But there are some electric heaters.

What you said to me about treating my children as if they were furniture or luggage was wicked and unjust. You tell me what else I could do. I'm doing what other women do when they get separated. The children have to stay with me, and I have to stay with I.F. in Rome. We are trying to sell *Le Margherite*. Piero has already found a little apartment in Perugia, near his office, and he will live there with his mother.

I can't sleep and at night I keep twisting and turning in bed, I put the light on then put it off, light up a cigarette then put it out, push all the pillows and blankets off the bed. My eyes seem to be full of pins. I'm not well. Roberta is very good to me. She is a great help to me. I talk a lot, I do nothing but talk.

The flat that was yours before is above my head. The Lanzaras live there. We went there for tea once. Your flat has been so changed that you wouldn't recognize it. What used to be the sitting-room is now a bedroom with chenille bedspreads in it. That's where I broke the ashtrays, remember?

My life has reached a turning point. This is why I can't sleep. I'm a bit annoyed with I.F. because he took it into his head to go off to Paris at such an important moment for us. And just when we have to look for a flat.

One thing about him has astonished me. He hasn't said that he would give me the money to buy a house, seeing that the money I have isn't enough. If he had offered it to me I'd have refused. But to tell you the truth I expected him to offer it to me, but he hasn't done so. And he's rich too. I think he's rich. But he and I never talk about money.

He doesn't want to leave his house in via della Scrofa. He pays according to the fair rent laws, and it's convenient. It's too small for us all to stay there, it's virtually just one room. Besides, he hasn't offered.

I'll have some money when we've sold *Le Margherite*. But I shall have to put some aside for living expenses. Piero will give whatever's necessary to support the children.

I think I'm pregnant. I get morning sickness. I don't want an abortion. I shall have a sixth child. It is I.F.'s. But I.F. is in Paris and doesn't know about it yet.

I want this sixth child. You know how much I like being pregnant. And I wanted to have a child with I.F. I told him I wanted to have a child with him. He didn't say anything. Sometimes he becomes extraordinarily silent, and I think he'll never talk to me again.

Serena has got back from Russia. She is in Pianura. On Saturday I shall go over and start emptying the place, room by room. Serena will help me. I get dizzy just thinking about it. *Le Margherite* is a big house, and full of things. I loved it so much once. Now I hate it.

I can't bear the country any more. I want a city around me: Rome.

We've already got a buyer for *Le Margherite*. He has offered two hundred million. Piero says it's not enough. He wants two hundred and fifty. They're discussing it.

My mother-in-law's at *Le Margherite* and she spends every day crying. When I go there she follows me from room to room and cries. She asks me if I won't reconsider, out of love for the children. I try to be kind to her, but I can't bear her.

The children are still at my sister-in-law's, in Forte die Marmi. They have missed more than a month of school. Never mind.

Piero and I now only talk about practical things. About possessions and money. How to divide the furniture, the crockery and the silver. Sometimes Piero also talks about me, He does this particularly when he phones. He starts out in a cold, calm tone and then little by little his voice gets thick and harsh. Then I ask him however he managed to live with me all this time, if he sees me as such a hypocrite and so faithless.

You've no idea how many things there are in a house. Too many. It seems impossible to have bought so much. It seems impossible to have bought all those things, and with such pleasure too. At the moment when I have to choose whether to leave things or take them with me I hate them all.

I met your son on the landing the other day. He recognized me and offered me his cold hand. He was going to the Lanzaras'. He's being psychoanalysed. Roberta says I should be psychoanalysed too because I'm at a difficult moment in my life. Perhaps she's right.

What a small world – your son is being psychoanalysed in the very flat you once owned.

Yours

Lucrezia

ROBERTA TO GIUSEPPE

Rome, 10th October

Dear Giuseppe,

Lucrezia gave me her letter to you to post. I'll add a few words of my own. Poor Lucrezia. She says she's happy, but to me she seems tired and lost. She's very pale. But then she's always pale. She says that she might be pregnant. I'd be desperate and would have an abortion immediately.

Piero phones in the evenings from Monte Fermo. These phone calls last for hours. Goodness knows how much that poor devil spends on long-distance calls. Luckily it's always him who calls, not Lucrezia, otherwise goodness knows how much I'd be spending.

I.F. phones too, but not so often, and not at such great length. He's phoned maybe three times since Lucrezia's been here.

I'm helping her to find a flat; we have seen a great many but she doesn't like any of them. Now she's going to stay in an apartment someone is lending her – it's not bad, a bit dark.

I feel sorry for the children.

With love from

Roberta

GIUSEPPE TO LUCREZIA

Princeton, 20th October

Dear Lucrezia,

I'm sending this letter to Monte Fermo. I imagine you are there now, packing everything up.

You wrote to me that your life has reached a turning point. My life has also reached a turning point. I'm getting married. I'm marrying Anne Marie, my brother's widow.

I wanted to let you know immediately. I wanted you to be one of the first people to know.

With love from

Giuseppe

ALBERICO TO GIUSEPPE

Rome, 10th November

Respected father,

I heard from Roberta that you have got married. I'm pleased. I know you've phoned to tell everyone – Roberta, and even Egisto. You didn't phone me though. I found that strange.

I am well. The baby is growing well. My life is pretty uneventful. They've accepted the screenplay for my film and I've been paid for it. I shall direct it. I think the film will be dreadful. But I enjoyed myself well enough thinking it up, and I think I'll enjoy myself making it.

In via Nazario Sauro a few days ago I met that friend of yours on the stairs, the woman who has the house in the country and all those children. I thought she'd become ugly and worn out; her eyes had dark circles round them. I think she's called Ophelia, or something like that.

Alberico

GIUSEPPE TO ALBERICO

Princeton, 18th November

Dear son,

I phoned you but you weren't at home. A woman's voice answered. She talked half in English and half in Italian. Clearly she forgot to tell you.

I'm sending you a little photograph of Anne Marie and me together in our garden. Mrs Mortimer, our next-door neighbour, took it.

Anne Marie is a very intelligent woman. She works in an Institute for Scientific Research. That is, she works on something I understand nothing whatsoever about. And I'm working on something she understands nothing whatsoever about. I'm writing a novel in Italian, a language she doesn't know.

Our days are spent in two separate worlds that have nothing to do with each other. We meet in the evenings, in the kitchen, and each of us says something about what we've done during the day, but very little for fear of boring the other. In living with someone else boredom is the worst risk.

Boredom appears when each person knows everything about the other, or thinks he knows everything about the other, and no longer gives a damn about it. But no, I'm wrong. No one knows why boredom appears.

My brother's and Anne Marie's marriage was based on interests held in common. Ours is based on the distance between my world and hers.

Don't think I'm not astonished to have married her. I feel astonished about it every day. I don't know if she wonders why she has married me. I still don't know.

She smiles all the time. She's one of those people who smiles all the time. At first I used to smile too, in answer to her. But I thought that at a certain point we would both stop smiling. I've stopped. But she hasn't, she smiles from when she gets up in the morning to when we go to bed in the evening.

I'm very pleased about what you told me concerning the film.

With love from

your father

SERENA TO EGISTO

Pianura, 28th November

Dear Egisto,

Perhaps you will have heard that Albina's mother has died. Perhaps she has phoned you or written to you. She is in a right mess now. Her father can't live alone. He's old, he's ill and he's deaf. Her sisters are very young. Her brother can only be bothered with his own affairs. An aunt was helping them but she has left. Albina will have to stay in Luco dei Marsi now. She has had to give up that job she had in Rome at the convent school. I shall have her bedsit.

I'm leaving Pianura. I'm sorry because I've become fond of the area. I've been there a few years now. But there isn't anyone at Monte Fermo now. *Le Margherite* is up for sale, and it doesn't make sense for me to stay here any more. For me, living in Pianura meant being near Piero and Lucrezia, seeing them every day. But what will I do in Pianura by myself? I shall go to Rome, that way I'll be company for Lucrezia. Lucrezia, if you ask me, has got herself into real trouble. She's done everything too quickly. She's sick of Piero, she can't stand him any longer. But then they had an open relationship, or so they said. People with an open relationship don't separate, each one comes and goes as he pleases.

Lucrezia is deceiving herself about Ignazio Fegiz. She imagines that this is her great love and that he is the one man in her life. Like hell he is. He hasn't gone to live with her and I don't believe he ever will. He wouldn't dream of it. And so she's alone and pregnant with five children and a dog in a dark, noisy apartment in the old part of Rome – without a blade of grass in sight or even a balcony, with a cleaning woman who's paid hourly, with hardly any money and hardly any freeedom to go out. It's a disaster.

Piero has moved to Perugia with Signora Annina. Just imagine the joy of having his mother under his feet all day. She even follows him to the office, because she doesn't know what to do with herself.

But it was good being with Piero and Lucrezia. Remember? It was good being with them both whether or not they had an open relationship. I mustn't think about it, because before I know where I am I'll start crying.

I'll tell you about my Russian trip. It was wonderful. We haven't seen each other since then. We haven't seen each other for ages.

I'm coming to Rome and I hope I'll see you a few times.

I've closed the Women's Centre, even so I have to pay the rent for a year, until the contract runs out.

Yours,

Serena

LUCREZIA TO GIUSEPPE

Rome, 12th December

Dear Giuseppe,

So, you're married. I'm not surprised because it was very clear from your recent letters that you were considering the idea.

I ought to congratulate you. I can't because this marriage of yours doesn't make me feel in a congratulatory mood at all. I keep all your letters. I keep them in my wardrobe in a cardboard box. Every now and then I get them out and look at them. How you hated Anne Marie when you arrived in America, and then later too, all the time your brother was alive. 'We haven't anything to say to each other in any language', 'I can't stand either her long neck, or her clear squinting eyes, or her smile, or her plait, or her bun.' I'm picking out phrases from your letters at random.

Roberta says that when you and your brother were children, you always wanted to do what he did. And so now you've married his wife. But I think you've finished up in a real stinking mess. I've seen a photograph of you and Anne Marie. Roberta showed it to me. Anne Marie is ugly. Those eyes, that raincoat, that smile. She's cross-eyed. Her smile is false. You have your usual look of a bird that's just fallen off a roof.

I'm fine. I'm in Rome, in an apartment someone's lent me, in Piazza del Paradiso. I see Roberta a lot. She is a great help to me. I see Serena who has come to live in Rome, in Albina's bedsit. Albina is at Luco dei Marsi. Her mother's died.

My apartment is a bit dark. I'm cold. I've bought some more electric heaters. There were already three of them, but I feel the cold a great deal.

However, the children are happy, and they like Rome. Vito goes to a kindergarten run by nuns. Cecilia takes him and picks him up. I feel sick all the time. My new baby will be born in April.

I brought one of the dogs, Joli, with me because the children liked him a lot. I gave the other dogs to the help at *Le Margherite*.

Piero comes to see us quite often. Relations between us are calm now. He phones before he comes because he doesn't want to bump into 'I'. I call him 'I' now. Even the children call him 'I'. Once however, 'I' and Piero did bump into each other. It didn't go too badly. First they talked about the price of houses, then about the price of pictures.

'I' hasn't come to live here yet. He's coming but not at the moment. He has to think things over for a while.

He usually eats lunch with us. At supper time he has to go to her place, to Ippo's. It's a relationship that's gone on for twenty years and he can't just break it off in one fell swoop. And she, Ippo, has a bad heart. My God, what a bloody nuisance she is. She has a bad stomach and she has a bad heart. I, on the other hand, am as strong as a horse. She has such a bad stomach and she can't eat. She has a horror of getting fat, and because of this she stopped eating years ago and this has made her stomach shrink. A carrot, a glass of hot water with a slice of lemon in it – that's what her meals are. 'I' has to go to her house every evening to see that she at least eats her carrot. Ippo. All day her name goes round and round inside my head. What with 'I' and Ippo I feel that *i* is the only letter in the alphabet.

I asked 'I' if Ippo knows that I am pregnant. He said yes, she knows. But he says very little about her to me. Before, I used to ask lots of questions about her, and he answered me to some extent. Now he doesn't answer, so I've stopped. I keep all these questions inside me now. They swell my belly up, like the baby.

I don't sleep well at night. I'm always waiting for 'I' to phone me, or I'm waiting for the noise of the lift and his key. He doesn't always come. Sometimes he phones me at one in the morning, worn out, really worn out, from via della Scrofa. It's difficult to get back to sleep, to find reassuring thoughts that will make me sleep.

Yours

Lucrezia

LUCREZIA TO GIUSEPPE

Rome, 15th December

I'll tell you about my new home.

It is L-shaped. There's a coat-stand in the entrance hall, not one that's fixed on the wall, but one of those you can move about, with lots of arms; it was black but I've painted it red. The living-room is long and narrow. I've put the Persian carpet in there, and the picture with the two coaches, and a sofa that I've had recovered. Piero kept the picture of King Lear. I've put the chest of drawers with the tortoises and the green wardrobe in my room. Daniele, Augusto and Graziano have a room with bunk-beds in it. There's another room with two beds where Cecilia and Vito sleep. I have put the quilts with dragons on these two beds. There's another little room next to my room and that will be for the new baby. Cecilia is fed up with sleeping with Vito and wants to sleep alone. She says I ought to give her the little room and have the new baby sleep in with me. But I don't want babies in my room. Cecilia and I argue about this all day long. She comes and sits herself down in front of me and tells me all the mistakes I made during the move. According to her, I have arranged the furniture and the rooms wrongly. She looks at me severely and I look at her in the same way. I think she's grown ugly. Her eyebrows have become bushy and her nose is swollen. She still has her lovely chestnut curls. But she's got fat and she always wears the same tight-fitting tartan dress. At the moment my relations with Cecilia are very bad. Cecilia doesn't love 'I' and misses her father. She doesn't say so, but when she sits in front of me and reproaches me for the chaos here, and for the furniture which according to her I've scattered all over the place, I know only too well what her real reproaches – which she hides and doesn't mention – are. I tell her she'll have a room of her own in our real new house, the one I'm buying. She answers that I'm not buying any real house. It's true. Sometimes I read the advertisements in *Il Messaggero*, but I imagine the houses in those advertisements to be extremely ugly, and then I feel unhappy, as if I were already living in one of them. And I'm very tired too. I'll go house-hunting after the baby is born.

As soon as I get up in the morning I put my fur coat on and go down to shop at the market in Campo dei Fiori, with Joli. This is quite a happy moment. I bought the fur coat second-hand in a shop near here. It's a long, yellow and black coat, made of German wolf fur. I'm not tired in the morning and I feel strong. I usually meet Serena because her bedsit, or rather Albina's bedsit, is near here, in via dei Sediari. Serena says to me, 'You're so big you look like a tower coming towards me.' 'And in fact I'd much rather be a little woman,' I answer. 'Little and very thin, around seven stone,' she says. I turn my face away because there are some things I don't like talking about. I don't like talking about Ippo. She takes my arm and we go between the stalls, I in my fur coat and she in her jacket made from African ram's wool. Then we have a cappuccino in a bar. I get on with Serena when she doesn't tell me about the mistakes I've made. At the moment everyone tells me about the mistakes I've made: Serena, Cecilia, Egisto (who came to see me one evening). After the market Serena helps me to carry the bags up. I don't ask her to stay for lunch because 'I' comes for lunch and relations between 'I' and Serena are very bad. I don't even ask her to come to supper because though 'I' isn't usually there, it could turn out that he is. So when Serena takes herself off she's always slightly offended. She eats alone in a pizzeria. She doesn't see many people. Egisto is having an affair with an American girl who is living with your son Alberico. She was supposed to be leaving, but she hasn't left yet. She is called Anais. I start cooking. I've a woman I pay by the hour who comes in to help. She's pretty unpleasant and I want to change her. She's called Enzina. She says she doesn't know how to cook but she hangs about while I am cooking and tells me all the mistakes I'm making. Then 'I' arrives. This is a very beautiful moment, perhaps the most beautiful of all. It doesn't last long, because almost immediately I'm afraid that something in the house is going to upset him – Enzina's face, or the smell of cauliflower, or the record-player which doesn't work properly. I was never afraid with Piero. Fear is a new thing for me. Usually 'I' sits in the living-room and puts records on while I finish preparing the lunch. I don't know, he seemed to love cooking when I first met him, but he never comes in the kitchen now. I don't understand why. I sit in the living-room with him and wait for the children. I'm on tenterhooks because he keeps looking at the time and the children are always late. He was so friendly to the children before, but now he and the children hardly speak. This upsets me a lot. We – 'I' and I – spend a few hours together in the afternoon. Sometimes we go to via della Scrofa and there we can be undisturbed. But Ippo's paintings are there. There are lots of pictures but I only see Ippo's, and I find them incredibly ugly, they are all a carroty red. I'm not always able to go to via della Scrofa with him because sometimes I have to go and pick up Vito from the kindergarten and take him for a walk when Cecilia says she has too much homework and can't go. She often says this, perhaps to stop me from going to via della Scrofa.

I think I'll get rid of Enzina and take on a woman from Capo Verde. I've met her and talked to her, but she isn't free yet, I have to wait. I'm always having to wait for something.

When I imagined my life in Rome, I imagined it so differently. I believed that 'I' would be living with me. Then suddenly he can't, I'm always asking him about it and he gets angry, he says I don't understand because I don't want to understand, it's suddenly completely impossible. Later. Later but when? He doesn't know.

I wish Ippo would die. It would be enough if he would leave her but he says he can't and then I wish she would die. He says I shouldn't say such terrible things and I shouldn't even think them. Perhaps I could manage not to say them but how can I not think them? What can anyone do against their thoughts? They crawl about your body, backwards and forwards, like worms or like diseases.

Lucrezia

GIUSEPPE TO LUCREZIA

Princeton, 28th December

Dear Lucrezia,

I wish you a happy Christmas, even though Christmas is over.

I received your letter. It depressed me. To tell you the truth I don't think 'I' is ever going to live with you. It's not so simple to live with five children, and soon there'll be six, when you are not used to it. 'I' has acted badly because he didn't tell you at once that this would be difficult for him and perhaps impossible. I was more honest with you.

The really bad thing is that he hasn't left that woman he's with. I've never seen this woman. I've seen her pictures in 'I's house in via della Scrofa. Her pictures seemed fairly ugly to me too, if that makes you feel any better.

Anne Marie and I spent Christmas alone, but yesterday Anne Marie's daughter, Chantal, arrived with her baby in her arms, She has left her husband. We knew there were difficulties between them. She arrived from Philadelphia at nine in the evening without having let us know she was coming. There had been a violent row. Chantal says that he hit her. She pulled up the sleeve of her dress and showed us a bruise on her arm. She's going to ask for a divorce. Something similar to what happened to her mother has happened to her. Anne Marie's first marriage also broke down suddenly. Anne Marie also left her husband with her baby in her arms.

Anne Marie wants me to go to Philadelphia to talk to Danny. I don't want to do this at all because I shall have to interrupt work on my novel and because I don't like being away from the house. But I shall have to do it.

Anne Marie smiles all the time. Chantal almost never smiles. Things are difficult between mother and daughter, as they are between you and Cecilia. They also argue all day. They argue savagely but very quietly. They never raise their voices, neither of them.

The baby is very pretty. Her name is Margaret, but she gets called Maggie. The baby and Chantal sleep in the room with the bear-cubs.

Write to me soon. Tell me how things are with you.

Giuseppe

LUCREZIA TO GIUSEPPE

Rome, 6th January

Dear Giuseppe,

I spent Christmas and the New Year at Terminillo, in a hotel, with Serena and the children. Piero was to have come but he caught influenza and stayed in Perugia.

'I' left for Paris before the holidays began and he hasn't come back yet.

Serena and the children went skiing at Terminillo. I went for little walks with Joli. We had taken Joli along. Which was a bad idea because they couldn't stand dogs in the hotel.

I went for little walks, very short, never going very far from the hotel. I was afraid that 'I' would phone me and they wouldn't be able to find me. Also I have a big belly now and I was afraid of slipping in the snow.

I spent hours stretched out on a deck chair on the terrace in front of the hotel. I did some knitting. Knitting is good for the nerves – I think your Mrs Mortimer said as much.

For a while now I've done nothing but wait. I wait for 'I' to phone me. I wait for my child to be born. I wait for my life to become less confused. Waiting gets on one's nerves. If you're waiting for a child to be born you shouldn't be waiting for anything else.

What an awful place Terminillo is. Windy, and full of stupid people. Serena chose it. She likes it. She enjoyed herself and so did the children. They ate like wolves, and so did I come to that. In the evenings we played *dubito*. It's a card game that children like. But then when we were alone in our room Serena started to say unpleasant things to me. She said I was wrong about everything. The separation, the house in Rome, everything. According to Serena 'I' doesn't care about me very much. This child I'm going to have won't have a father. He will have Piero's surname, certainly Piero won't deny paternity. But after that he'll be a child without a father. 'I' won't even look at him. He will say he isn't his. According to Serena he will do what you did over Graziano, just the same. Except that Piero accepted Graziano as his, but I hadn't broken the marriage up then and now on the other hand I have broken it up, and I've got myself in a real fucking mess. According to Serena men are bastards, all except for Piero who is an angel and I have been a complete idiot to leave him. I left him to be with 'I' who is the worst bastard of the lot. I got undressed and got under the blankets and turned my face to the wall and she walked up and down the room and then I saw her face hanging over me all smothered in cream, and we both started to cry.

Now we are back in Rome. Piero came to see us for a day; he brought lots of presents for the children, and a shawl for me.

Yours

Lucrezia

ROBERTA TO GIUSEPPE

Rome, 9th January

Dear Giuseppe,

I went and talked to Ignazio Fegiz, or to 'I' as Lucrezia calls him. I didn't say anything to Lucrezia, I just went. I thought that as I don't like him and he probably doesn't like me, we wouldn't run any risk of spoiling our relationship, seeing that it was so bad to begin with. I phoned him, put my fur coat on and got into my little Fiat 500. It was snowing. Unfortunately the Fiat stopped at Largo Argentina. I had to go quite a way on foot, walking through the snow and mud.

Our discussion was cold, calm, and at the same time inconclusive. I don't understand that man. He seems to be open but in fact he's as closed as an oyster. As far as I can see he's already tired of Lucrezia. And now he doesn't know how to free himself from her. I told him that he should be clearer with Lucrezia. That when a woman messes up her whole life for love she deserves at least a little honesty. He responded with great gestures of assent. I asked him if he intended to give his name to the baby that was going to be born. He said there was no doubt at all of that. Then he started to explain to me that all the same, he found himself in a delicate situation. He has an old attachment. A sick, a very sick woman. It is a deep and very close attachment. In a certain sense it is no different from a matrimonial attachment. And so he has to move very, very cautiously. I told him that it seemed to me that he was using this person to shield himself from other weightier responsibilities. He blushed, he blushed a great deal. He said that perhaps, in a certain sense, I could be said to be right. But how rash, how impulsive, Lucrezia is, he said. An unbroken horse. She never thinks of others, she thinks only of herself. She drags those children about as if they were so much luggage. He felt sorry for those children. He felt sorry for Piero too. He felt sorry for everyone, I said, except Lucrezia. No, he said, he felt sorry for Lucrezia too. He wanted her to be happy. How, I said, if she's happy only when she's with him and he's both there and not there. Finally I asked him if he was in love with her. This was the essential thing I had to ask him but it was only at the end that I dragged it out of him. He said that he loved her very much. Then he looked at the time and I realized I had to go. He put his raincoat on and that peaked cap he wears, and came out with me. I must say I didn't entirely dislike him when he was walking along the street. He strides along quickly and has a cheerful air about him. He walked to Largo Argentina with me and helped me push the car till it started. Then I saw that he went off to his olive-green Renault which was parked in corso Vittorio.

Your son is well. He's still going upstairs for his psychoanalysis. He goes, but he's started to say that as far as he can see, this Lanzara fellow is a bit stupid. Pleasant, a fine person, but a bit stupid. I asked him if he told him he thought he was stupid. I know you have to tell psychoanalysts everything. He said that he tells him the whole time. Lanzara doesn't take offence. Psychoanalysts never take offence.

Alberico told me that soon, perhaps next spring, his film *Deviance* will be shown in Rome. Why don't you come on a trip to Italy, with Anne Marie, next spring, to visit Alberico and all our friends, and our dear miss-matched Lucrezia, and to see the film?

With love from

Roberta

EGISTO TO ALBINA

Rome, 15th January

Dear Albina,

Yesterday Anais left. I must say I'm sorry. I'll miss her. I was fond of her. In the end she was living with me. She said there was too much of a mess downstairs. Yesterday Alberico and I took her to the airport. She had been saying she had to leave for a while, but she stayed on nevertheless.

Our relationship lasted for exactly five months. I didn't mean anything to her and it wasn't for me that she stayed on in Rome. She had other men besides me and she told me about them in a quite unemotional way. She had a builder in Parioli, then a Chilean painter. Sometimes she didn't come back at night. I sleep easily but when I didn't see her come back I worried and couldn't sleep. She would come back in the morning whilst I was getting dressed to go to the newspaper. Once she had a row with the builder and came back crying. She had stolen some money from him and he had hit her. She stole things. She was a millionaire but she stole things. She stole because she enjoyed stealing. I couldn't go into a supermarket with her because she always slipped something into her handbag – perfume, or a box of biscuits. She was as quick as a monkey. But she never stole anything from me. She took drugs. According to her, everyone in the flat downstairs takes drugs. I don't know if that's true or not. She talked about great quantities of the stuff. I never tried to preach to her, either about men, or about her pilfering, or about drugs. It seemed useless to me. She wasn't especially beautiful, you saw her in the restaurant that day. But I'd got used to her. I was fond of her. Now I'm alone again.

Whilst we were coming back from the airport yesterday Alberico noticed that I was a bit sad and invited me to have supper at their place. I don't mind being in all that mess. I sit down and do everything as if it weren't there. I put a record on, play with the baby a bit. The baby is in her play-pen and she walks a little, hanging on to the bars, then falls down and cries a little. Nadia either sleeps or eats or cries or reads magazines. Nadia cries a lot, either because something's hurting her or because she's afraid of something or because of an upsetting thought that has come to her or because of a dream she's had. Salvatore either sleeps or bustles about in the kitchen. However, he's a bit fed up with cooking and they often get food sent up from the restaurant underneath, *Il Fagiolaro*. There are always people coming and going, friends of Alberico who come and see him about the film. They run errands for him or find things he needs. Antique soup-tureens, pieces of cloth. He sits at his typewriter and gives orders. He's like a general. There are always two or three of these people there when they eat. After they've eaten they stay at the table in the kitchen for a long time. No one says much. They smoke joints. I smoke them with them so as not to seem old-fashioned.

I miss you a lot. I didn't feel it so much when Anais was here but now that Anais has gone I want to chat to you and eat with you occasionally. I go to Lucrezia's every now and then but I don't know if she likes to see me. I don't know if that 'I' of hers is around or not. I phone her before I go. I took Anais once. They liked each other well enough. Afterwards Lucrezia told me that Anais has a certain stylishness, but that she's cold and dry. Anais told me that she thought Lucrezia was like a pregnant elephant.

I see Serena sometimes. She has reduced your bedsit to a wretched state. You walk over plates, newspapers and jumpers. Serena is very happy because she has met a director, called Umberto. This director and Serena have become friends and have decided to put on Alfieri's *Mirra*.

Try to come and see me, if it's possible for you. Or I'll come to Luco. It doesn't matter if you don't have anywhere to put me up. I can sleep in a hotel.

Egisto

ALBINA TO EGISTO

Luco dei Marsi, 22nd January

I'm getting married, Egisto.

I'm marrying Nino Mazzetta. He makes reproduction antique furniture. The factory, the shop, and also the house where he lives are in a courtyard behind my house. The furniture is well-made, though it doesn't seem antique, it's shiny and has a new look about it. Nino Mazzetta is a widower with a nine-year-old son. The son is doing badly at school and he brings his homework over to me. Nino Mazzetta works hard but he's not rich and he's paying off debts.

I'm marrying him for the following reasons, which I have carefully thought over one by one. Because I want to have children. Because I'm already thirty-three. To please my father. Because I'll be able to continue to run my house until my sisters are grown up, as there's only a courtyard between Mazzetta's house and mine. Because no one's ever thought of marrying me, but Nino Mazzetta has. Because he's a good person. Whenever my father asked him to lend him money he has always done so. When my brother asked him to lend him money he gave it to him and he's never got it back again, but he doesn't mind and he's continued to come to our house from time to time, in the evening after supper, and he plays cards with my father and chats to him even though chatting with my father is not an easy matter because you have to repeat the same thing to him ten times. Because I am poor. When I marry I shan't be rich, but I shall be less poor. Because my life is very wearisome in Luco and I think that if I'm not mistaken, it'll be easier when I'm married.

Nino Mazzetta is marrying me for the following reasons, which he spelt out to me one by one. Because he doesn't find me ugly. Because I have simple habits. Because I don't intimidate him even though I'm an arts graduate and he only reached the fifth class in elementary school. His dead wife intimidated him even though she had only reached the third class in elementary school. She was a quarrelsome person and they weren't happy together. Because I play the flute. Because I cook badly and he likes to eat well but he thinks that with a cookery book I'll learn quickly. Because he's known me since I was little. Because he knows my family well.

I've known him since I was little too, but this doesn't make me all that happy. I feel that my future was already fated and mapped out for me.

Last September I went to the *Unitá* festival. He was there too and he asked me to have supper with him. We ate grilled sausages at a table under some trees. Then we went home. I think the idea of getting married to me came to him that evening.

He likes talking and he talks a lot. He talks about his life and ideas. I stay quiet. He never asks me questions. And so he knows almost nothing about me. He doesn't know that I went with boys, in Rome, when I had my bedsit. He doesn't know that bed is a problem for me. I went with three boys in all: an English student who was a friend of Serena's, someone I kept meeting on the bus, and someone who sold encyclopaedias. They aren't happy memories. Those boys didn't amount to much. The best was perhaps the bus one, but he was from Palermo and he went back to Palermo after a week. He sent me postcards a few times. I was happy in my bedsit, that's certainly true. What a pity I've lost it. But then, how could I have kept it. I couldn't have left my father. I liked living in Rome and going to *Le Margherite* on Saturdays, and talking to Serena about the Women's Centre. And now *Le Margherite* no longer exists. I heard that some priests had bought it and that it's going to be used by a religious community. The Women's Centre no longer exists. I phone Lucrezia sometimes and she answers in a curt, hurried way. Serena has been to see me a couple of times. She saw Nino Mazzetta from the window. He seemed short and uncouth to her. You've never been to see me, otherwise I'd have introduced you to him and you could have advised me. But to tell the truth I wouldn't have listened to you much.

We are getting married in a month. We are getting married in church even though we are not religious – neither he nor I. My father isn't religious either, but he wants it like that.

I shall have quite a beautiful outfit, of pale blue gaberdine, it's a skirt and top which the seamstress in the courtyard has made for me.

We haven't had any kind of sexual relationship. We are never alone because my father thinks it's better to follow the old ways and when we go out in the evening there's always my brother, Maura and Gina there too. So I haven't been able to tell Nino Mazzetta anything about myself and anyway he talks continuously to my brother and me.

My brother says I'm selfish and sly and that he'd never have thought it of me. He says that Nino Mazzetta will make pots of money with his rotten furniture even if he is up to his eyes in debt at the moment.

Nino Mazzetta has very white hair and a very black moustache. He is short and chain-smokes. Sometimes he can't sleep at night through thinking about his debts and then he gets up and makes himself a cup of hot milky coffee. That's what he told my brother and me.

Everything would be fine if bed were not such a problem for me.

Albina

EGISTO TO ALBINA

Rome, 28th January

You are about to do something really silly, Albina.

Forget it. Forget the lot, the pale blue gaberdine outfit, the shop, the milky coffee, the courtyard. Or at least wait. Wait for a year. In a year something will happen. You can find a good job in Rome, pay someone to be with your father and come away from that wretched place for good. There are lots of solutions, and the one you have chosen is the worst.

I'll come and see you as soon as I can, and I'll argue you out of this stupid marriage in which your future is fated and all mapped out for you.

Egisto

GIUSEPPE TO LUCREZIA

Princeton, 2nd February

Dear Lucrezia,

I've finished my novel. A student on my course has typed it up for me. I asked her if she liked it and she said she found it interesting. She is the only person who has read it and unfortunately she's a stupid girl. Anne Marie and Chantal don't know Italian.

I went to New York a few days ago. I went to see Danny but I thought that I could also look for either a translator or a literary agent. I had the address of a cousin of Mrs Mortimer's who knows a great many people and might be able to advise me. So I put a copy of the novel in my briefcase. But my main reason for going was to see Danny and talk to him about the divorce. I don't know if you remember that Danny is Chantal's husband. I told you about him. Anne Marie wanted me to go and see him in Philadelphia but when I phoned him he said that he would be going to New York on business and that I could meet him there.

I arranged to meet him in that hotel where I stayed when I arrived in America. It's called the Continental Hotel and it's on Fifth Avenue. I booked a room. It was a very similar room to the one I had when I was ill and stayed in bed and my brother sat with me. And so while I was waiting for Danny I became very miserable. Danny was late. I tried to phone Mrs Mortimer's cousin but there was an answering machine at the other end. I started to re-read my novel. It didn't seem bad to me. It is called *The Knot*. I won't tell you about it. I've sent you a copy.

Danny finally arrived. I immediately opened the fridge and poured him a big glass of whisky. Danny drinks a lot. I thought I would have to convince him that a divorce was the only possible solution. But he was already convinced of that. When Chantal left the house with the baby he thought that she would never come back. He'd thought it with a sense of relief because recently their life together had been terrible. Danny is small, he has red hair and jug ears and little, sharp teeth like a mouse's. We stayed in that room for a long time. He drank a great many glasses of whisky. He told me about his childhood. He had already told me in Princeton, and in New York he told me again. He doesn't have any parents. He was born in a foundling hospital. He has changed family five times. He has stayed very close to one of these families, the last but one. Their name is Pippolo and they are of Italian origin. They live in Baltimore. They are poor and have lots of children. He helps them. He and Chantal also argued about that. According to Chantal the Pippolo family are bloodsuckers. She worked herself into a frenzy over the Pippolo family. She's hard-hearted, Chantal is. I said that on the contrary she seemed to me to be a sweet girl. He said I was making a big mistake. All Chantal's and the baby's clothes are still in their apartment in Philadelphia. He will send them on to Princeton as soon as he can. He will come and see the baby now and then and in the holidays he will take her to Baltimore, to the Pippolos' that is to his only real family. He had never hit Chantal. He had simply seized her arm a little too roughly that evening. She had immediately called a neighbour and begged her to come with her to a clinic, where they found a tiny bruise. Then she came home and thrust her night-cream and the baby's pyjamas into a bag. She thought about her night-cream but she didn't think about the baby's vitamins, she's left them there. Next morning she phoned from Princeton and told him to send all her things at once. He hadn't done so yet because having to collect together and send off all those clothes was too tiring and upsetting for him.

I suggested we go out and have dinner. I remembered a Chinese restaurant I'd been to with my brother and we went there. Over dinner he gradually calmed down. He asked me how I was. I told him I had finished my novel and that I had to find a translator and an agency. Later I'd also try to have it published in Italy, but as I was in America I'd be very happy if it came out in America. He told me that he had a friend in Philadelphia who knew Italian well and who had translated books, and he could either translate the novel or place it with an agency. He was sorry he couldn't read it himself because he didn't know Italian. Pippolo's mother had tried to teach him, but he'd only managed to remember a few words. However according to him the title was no good. There are already ten novels called *The Knot.* Then he started to talk about Chantal and their relationship again. She's a cold woman Chantal is. He had never understood Anne Marie but he had never liked her and he thought she must be a cold, dry woman like Chantal. Then I said I was ready to sleep and that it was already very late, and that anyway it was pointless to wallow in hatred and bitterness and melancholy like he did. He said I was right and that he had a real liking for me. I was similar in some ways to the Pippolos' eldest boy, who was his best friend. He thought he'd come to Princeton soon to see the baby and we'd have another opportunity to spend a few hours together. If I'd give him my novel in the meantime he would take it to Philadelphia, to the man who might translate it. We went back to my hotel, I gave him the novel and he stuffed it into his inside coat-pocket. We separated. An acquaintance of the Pippolos was putting him up for the night.

The next day I was in Princeton again. I reported my conversation with Danny and Anne Marie got angry. She said I'd acted like a fool. I should have talked about the divorce and not about anything else. I should have been severe, concise and distant. It was stupid of me to give him my novel, to accept a favour from him. When Anne Marie gets angry she doesn't stop smiling, but her mouth trembles and she gets red blotches on her face and neck. Chantal on the other hand did not get angry. She said that the main thing was that the clothes should arrive because neither she nor the baby had anything to wear. Then she suddenly burst out laughing. She said she found the idea of Danny and me sitting down and chatting away like old friends funny. Chantal almost never smiles, but every now and then she laughs, she bursts out into a shrill, high-pitched laugh that ends in a little sob. However, when I said that Danny intended to take the baby to the Pippolos' during the holidays she stopped laughing and said that she would not allow it because the Pippolos were coarse, dirty people. Then her mother said that there wasn't much to allow or not allow, and that Danny would do whatever he thought fit with the baby during the holidays.

As soon as you get the package with my novel in it let me know. I'd like you to read it soon. I'm impatient to know what you think of it.

Giuseppe

ROBERTA TO GIUSEPPE

Rome, 5th April

Dear Giuseppe,

Lucrezia's baby was born last Friday, but he only lived for two days. He was a fine looking boy. It has all been very sad.

I was with her the whole time. She had the first contractions and went into hospital and called me from there. She was alone, poor girl. 'I' took it into his head to go off to Paris just over those few days, and he was unreachable.

Lucrezia suffered a lot, it was a difficult birth. I phoned Piero in Perugia, I was worried and wanted someone to be there. Piero came immediately.

The baby was born and it seemed that everything was over. 'I' arrived. I had thought he was a bastard when he went off, but to tell the truth I stopped thinking so when I saw him. He's one of those people it's impossible to hate when you actually see them. He has that crew-cut and that energetic determined air about him, and at the same time looks bewildered. He liked the baby immensely and seemed happy.

Then we learnt that there was something wrong with the baby. It was an extremely sad afternoon, I shall never forget that Sunday afternoon. We were all there – me, Piero, 'I', Serena, even Cecilia. Serena had had the daft idea of bringing Cecilia along with her. I didn't think it was right that a little girl should be there at such a sad time. We had lost hope, but Lucrezia clung to the belief that nothing they said was true. The baby died at ten in the evening. I remained with Lucrezia throughout the night. A doctor on the ward told me I could stay.

Lucrezia is still in hospital and it'll be a few more days before she's able to come home.

If you want to phone her you can call her at home on Monday or Tuesday.

With love from

Roberta

LUCREZIA TO GIUSEPPE

Rome, 10th April

Dear Giuseppe,

Roberta told me that she had written to you and that you had phoned her, and so you already know what has happened to me.

I received your novel some time ago, but I can't read it at the moment. I can't even touch it. It's on my table, in its pale blue folder.

If you write to me, don't write as if you pitied me. I don't want people to feel pity for me. Perhaps I'd even prefer it if you didn't write to me at all for a while. Roberta says that you told her you would phone me. Don't. I don't want to hear your voice. I don't want voices.

Yours

Lucrezia

LUCREZIA TO GIUSEPPE

Rome, 25th April

Dear Giuseppe,

I was pleased when you phoned me the other day. I can't remember now what you said to me or what I answered. Nothing, or almost nothing. I could have pulled out the connection and taken the phone into my room, but instead I stayed in the living-room where Daniele and Cecilia were. Anyway, I was pleased that you phoned me. I thought I wouldn't be, but I was pleased. You didn't talk as if you pitied me and I thank you for that.

You said you thought of coming to Italy to see me, and perhaps you will come, but not just now. Goodness knows why not just now. In fact I don't think you'll come all that soon. You have planted your long, thin feet down over there, in Princeton.

I haven't read your novel yet. I don't read anything, not even the newspapers. I get up late and keep my dressing-gown on all day. I don't even go out to do the shopping. I have that woman from Capo Verde now, perhaps I've mentioned her to you. Egisto found her for me. In the morning she goes to your son's to look after that girl's baby. At noon she comes to me. She does the shopping and makes lunch. She is a fat, black woman, with a handkerchief on her head. She is called Zezé.

Yours

Lucrezia

LUCREZIA TO GIUSEPPE

Rome, 5th May

My baby was born on Friday 25th March at six in the afternoon. He died after two days. He died on Sunday evening.

I went to the hospital alone on Friday morning in the Volks wagen with the suitcase I had had ready for several days. Serena stayed at home to wait for the children and to make them lunch. 'I' was in Paris. He had told me that he had to meet some people about some pictures in Paris, but that he would come back straight away. I phoned him at his hotel in Paris on Friday morning but he wasn't there. I cursed him whilst I was in the Volkswagen. I was furious with him, but calm in myself. I thought that I had already given birth so many times and that it had always been a quick, easy process. I phoned Roberta from the hospital, just to have someone with me. She came at once.

By midday I felt very ill. I realized that it was a difficult birth. Roberta seemed worried to me, but she was trying not to let me see it. I cursed. Then I stopped cursing and called out for my mother. I didn't remember that she had been dead for years. I wanted Piero to be there. He had always been there when I gave birth and I wanted him there this time too. I don't know if I mentioned him. I can't remember now what I said and what I didn't say. I thought I was dying.

There was great confusion all around me. I couldn't see Roberta any more and I wasn't in the same room any more. Then they gave me injections and I didn't feel anything else.

When I came round the first face I saw was Piero's. Someone had phoned him, either Roberta or Serena, and he had come at once. They showed me the baby. He had long black hair. Piero said that he looked like Cecilia.

Then Piero left and after a while 'I' arrived. Roberta had

phoned him and he had caught a plane. He was pale. They took him to see the baby. He was very pleased with him. The baby was in a room at the end of the corridor with nine others. 'I' said he was the best of the nine, by far the best looking. He said that he looked like a Chinese magistrate. He resembled his father. He wanted him to be called Giovanni, like his father. All of a sudden he started to talk about his parents, about whom he never talks. They have been dead for many years. They had a chemist's shop in Ancona. The famous Fegiz Pharmacy. Roberta and Serena were in the room. When he went out of the room for a moment Serena whispered to Roberta that she couldn't stand him. I heard and said she could go if she couldn't stand him. She could go to my house and see what Zezé was doing. It was Zezé's first day there and everything had to be explained to her.

Then Piero came back and he brought me some roses. He and 'I' shook hands in a very friendly way. Roberta said that they had better go to the registrar to report the birth, and that Piero would have to disclaim paternity otherwise the baby would not be called Giovanni Fegiz but Giovanni Mantelli. 'I' started talking about his father Giovanni Fegiz again. He said there was lots of time to go to the registrar.

A nurse told us they had taken the baby out of the room where there were nine of them, and had put him in a room by himself because he wasn't breathing very well. We could still see him just the same, from the other side of a glass window, and 'I' went to see him and said that he was breathing marvellously. The nurse drew off some of my milk to give it to the baby with a dropper. He mustn't get too tired. He was healthy, just a little weak.

Serena came the next morning and told me there was something wrong with the baby. The doctors had told her. He didn't breathe well, he had a heart defect. I don't know why but Serena always gets a certain kick out of giving me bad news. She loves me a lot I know, nevertheless she likes being able to give me bad news. Her eyes light up with a strange glow. I felt heartbroken. I told Serena to go and call Roberta, but Roberta had gone home to sleep, Piero had gone to the Villa Borghese with the children and 'I' had disappeared too. A nurse scolded Serena for telling me things I shouldn't have been told.

Then Roberta and Piero arrived. Roberta told me that 'I' was in the waiting-room and that as soon as he saw a doctor going by he assailed him with thousands of questions. Well yes, there was something wrong. The baby had a small heart defect. But Roberta knew someone, the son of one of her friends, who had the same thing and was alive and well. He was strong and robust. The hours went by and I waited for them to tell me that everything was going well. Instead a doctor came and told me that there was little hope. 'I' was in the waiting room the whole time. He appeared in my room every now and then, sat down and then immediately jumped up; he suddenly started to yell that this hospital was a shit-house where nobody explained anything clearly. Piero took him to the cafeteria downstairs to have a coffee.

At ten in the evening they told us that the baby was dead.

I stayed in that hospital for many more days. 'I' came to see me. He stayed silent most of the time. He only mentioned the baby once. He told me that he had never realized that he wanted a son, but that when he saw the baby he understood that that was the one thing in the world that he really wanted. He told me that when he went to have a coffee with Piero that evening, they had talked for a long time and that he had felt very close to him. He told me that Piero was an extraordinary person, goodness only knew why I had left him. Women, he said, are real idiots. I thought it was dreadful of him to say such a thing, so dreadful that I told him to get out and that I never wanted to see him again. But instead he stayed sitting where he was, patting his hair, until the nurse came as she did every evening to give me a tablet and to tell him that he had to go as it was past nine o'clock.

The next day I told him something that I had been thinking about constantly all those days. I told him that I had so hated his way of always leaving me alone and that I had so hated Ippo that all this hatred had finished up in the baby's bloodstream and poisoned him. Or perhaps I had thought about Ippo so much that she had hidden herself away inside of me and infected the baby with her heart disease. He stood up and came towards my bed grinding his teeth. He told me that he could not forgive what I said. When he met me he had thought I was strong and generous. I wasn't. My soul was full of wretchedness and poison. He said this in a deep hoarse voice. Then he put his raincoat on and left. I stayed awake and cried all night, then he phoned me the next morning and came back again.

The baby was registered and buried with the name Giovanni Mantelli. Piero had not disclaimed paternity. By this time everyone thought it immaterial whether he had one surname or another.

I went home again. The room that should have been for the baby has become a guest room. Cecilia didn't want to come and sleep there. She says that sometimes Vito is afraid in the night and she has to have him in her bed. And then she had seen the baby, both from behind the window when he was with the other nine, and on the Sunday evening when he died. She says she can't forget him. If she slept in that room she would do nothing but dream about dead babies. Piero sleeps in that room when he comes to Rome. At first he used to go to a hotel, but I thought it was stupid for him to go to a hotel when there's a bed here. He turns up in Rome quite often because at the moment he has business in Rome. I've put a bed in the room, the grey carpet and the chest-of-drawers with the tortoises.

The days go by without my doing anything. I lie stretched out on the sofa, I look out of the window. I don't want anything, and sometimes I'm afraid that what happened to my mother will happen to me.

Everyone says to me: Pull yourself together. You already have lots of children. I know, but I wanted this one too.

Roberta comes to see me every day. She busies herself with the house a bit and keeps an eye on Zezé. Egisto often comes, but Serena rarely comes because she has rehearsals at the theatre. She is going to act in Alfieri's *Mirra* in a little theatre they've recently set up. Acting in *Mirra* has been the great dream of her life. She sleeps with the director, who is called Umberto. She's very happy about everything.

Yours

Lucrezia

GIUSEPPE TO LUCREZIA

Princeton, 27th April

Dear Lucrezia,

You have repeatedly told me you don't want pity. So I will just say that I think of you with great affection. I shall come to Italy soon. No, not at once. I have my course of lessons to give. I've various things to do, I shall have to see my translator and get his advice about an agency. But sooner or later I'll come, you'll see.

I think about you a lot. I talk about you to Chantal a lot, I also talked about you to Danny who has come to Princeton a few times to see his little girl. I never talk about you to Anne Marie because when I started telling her about you she said that she wasn't really interested in people she didn't know.

Chantal has now found a job in a tourist agency. She leaves the baby in a crêche and goes at four to pick her up. Sometimes when I don't have any lessons I go to pick her up. I take her to the park and Chantal meets us there. We spend hours in the park, and it's very peaceful there, with the huge trees and the squirrels and birds. Then we go back to the house and Chantal and I prepare supper together. When Anne Marie comes in it's already done. But she always finds fault with something. Anne Marie and Chantal start arguing almost immediately. It's always for some trivial reason, a dirty cup on the table in the hall, a half-eaten apple on an armchair, a blouse that's been used to wipe the floor with. Chantal is pretty disorganized and very absent-minded. Anne Marie becomes furious and mother and daughter exchange angry words in a whisper. I try and make peace but then Anne Marie gets annoyed with me, and our suppers often pass in silence. The baby is put to bed but she continually gets out of bed and comes in the kitchen and Anne Marie doesn't say anything but she fiddles with her fork and glass and her neck becomes covered in red blotches. Schultz and Kramer usually come after supper. Anne Marie calms down then and sits and chats with them in the living-room. Meanwhile Chantal and I clear up in the kitchen and put the baby to bed again, and she invariably gets up again. When she finally goes off to sleep we sit in the living-room too, with a glass of whisky, but Chantal gets bored and starts yawning, and I get bored too and suppress my yawns, until Schultz and Kramer go and Anne Marie scolds us because we weren't welcoming to them and if it goes on like this one evening they won't come any more.

I'd be very pleased if you'd like to read my novel one day – there's no hurry, there's all the time in the world. When Danny came here the last time, a few days ago, he said that his friend had already translated sixty pages or so and that he'd given them him to read, and that he had found it very interesting and was impatient to find out what happened next. The next time he comes here he might bring his friend, who is very keen to meet me and ask me about certain moments he hasn't understood. Danny doesn't want to see Chantal when he comes here, so I take the baby to his hotel, which is a pretty squalid little rooming-house because Danny hasn't much money and he has recently lost his job. I leave the baby with him and go back to pick her up and then we arrange to meet in the evening and we spend hours talking together. Anne Marie isn't happy about this, she doesn't say anything but she turns the corners of her mouth down and gives an exasperated little sigh. Perhaps Chantal isn't happy about this either, but she shrugs her shoulders and bursts out into a shrill laugh and says that everyone is free to spend his time with whoever he likes. Last time Danny asked me to lend him some money and I gave him some, but I didn't tell either Anne Marie or Chantal.

Danny and Chantal have begun divorce proceedings. According to Danny, Chantal won't be able to put up with living with her mother for long, and according to him she is already thinking of going off and living alone, maybe in New York. I asked Chantal if this were true and she told me it wasn't, that for the moment she would remain with us. If Chantal leaves I shall really miss her. The house is much more cheerful with Chantal and the baby here, and Chantal and I talk together a lot, and enjoy doing so, and when she is at work and I am at the school I amass a great heap of things in my mind that I want to tell her, and that I actually do tell her as soon as we are together again. She is a sweet girl, Chantal. She has her cold moments because her mother has always been too strict with her. Anne Marie isn't a motherly person. I told Anne Marie this and she said I was right. Mother and daughter can't stand each other. In fact, Anne Marie can't stand the baby either. She says she feels too old to have a baby in the house.

Send me your news.

Giuseppe

LUCREZIA TO GIUSEPPE

Rome, 20th May

I went to Vallombrosa for ten days, with 'I'. We got back four days ago. Roberta and Piero said I needed a change of air. 'I' came with me. He didn't want to at first, because he said he had lots of commitments in Rome. Then all of a sudden he decided to come and it was him who chose the hotel. A good hotel. He said he had a lot of money at the moment and that I needed all the comforts available, and so did he for that matter.

We set off in the olive-green Renault, which I hadn't been in for ages. Roberta moved into my place, to look after the house.

I put your novel in my suitcase. So I've finally read it. I enjoyed it.

What happened between you and me at Viterbo happened between 'I' and me at Vallombrosa. We said goodbye, it's over. With this difference, that at Viterbo it was me who said we had to finish, and at Vallombrosa he said it. And also with another difference, that at Viterbo you and I were both very sad, but calm underneath, and neither of us felt that we wouldn't see each other again. But at Vallombrosa we both felt that we had acted very badly, I to him and he to me, and that we should never see each other again for any reason whatsoever. Perhaps this didn't seem so terrible to him, but it seemed terrible to me because I think I'm still in love with him.

Egisto says that when he is with Ippo, Ippo talks and he stays quiet all the time. But I'd guess that his silence with Ippo is a beautiful thing. He was silent with me at the end and it was an ugly silence. I didn't talk either. We both felt worn-out and tired, and suddenly old. He stared into space and patted that grey crew-cut of his. I fiddled with my hair and gathered it all up on to the top of my head.

It rained the whole time at Vallombrosa. I read your novel while 'I' read some books he had brought with him. When I finished your novel I wanted to give it to him, but he said he couldn't read modern novels. He was reading Aeschylus' tragedies. When it stopped raining we went for walks in the woods. I remembered the walks he and I went for at Monte Fermo when we first got to know each other. Long strides. Long, beautiful silences, full of secret words. Sudden, silly bursts of laughter. Short, inconclusive phrases. Thoughts that got tangled up and went round in circles. Hair in my eyes. That constant sense of triumphant complicity. Now we walked separately, he in front and I behind. Every now and then he waited for me to catch up. He would sigh and then start walking again without turning round, with one hand in his pocket and the other behind his back. You remember he always keeps one hand behind his back. I followed on behind and wondered every now and then what was happening at home, if they'd remembered to take Joli out, if Cecilia was in a bad mood, and Vito was being difficult. I had an immense desire to go home, and at the same time I didn't want to go there at all. We went back to the hotel and I changed my shoes. In our room there were some dark pictures, of fruit and dead pheasant. We went down to have dinner in the dining-room, which was in a basement. I looked at the people at the other tables, he looked at the wall. At a certain point during dinner he would disappear, and I knew that he was telephoning. He came back and gave me a little twisted smile, moving just one corner of his mouth.

He said we had to finish with each other. And then all of a sudden we rediscovered our intimacy and a sense of complicity. But it was a complicity that was as heavy as a rock, and it's only use was to show us that there was no way we could go on. That's how we spent the last days together.

A French couple he knew arrived at the hotel, and he cheered up when he saw them. They knew Ippo and mentioned her. He went for a walk with them once. He tripped and twisted his ankle. He couldn't drive, and so I drove the Renault on the way back.

Now I'm at home. When I got home the children had measles. I asked Roberta to stay on for a few more days. She sleeps in the little room. She's going on Saturday because Piero's coming.

Being with people wears me out, but I get even more worn out when I'm alone. I find the children wearisome. They asked why in the world 'I' doesn't come to lunch any more. I told them he doesn't come because he's hurt his foot.

Egisto and Serena come and see me. They come out of pity because I don't entertain them, I don't say a word, and sometimes I treat them badly. I haven't told anyone that 'I' has left me but I think everyone has realized.

I had a lover and he left me. I feel ugly and old. My hair is falling out, I've got wrinkles. My face isn't pale any more, it's yellow. 'My splendid pallor' has gone.

Sometimes I think I'll never see you again, and I'm happy that this should be so, because I don't want you to see me as I am now. But at the same time I feel that perhaps you are the only person in the world I could be with without feeling exhausted.

As I told you, I enjoyed your novel. I think it's well written. But I didn't read it properly because I was thinking about myself as I read it. I didn't skip anything, not even the descriptions, but to tell you the truth I read just with my eyes, and my thoughts were elsewere. There are perhaps rather too many descriptions, and I can't bear descriptions in novels. Sometimes I thought you were spinning it out and not really saying anything. That character who experiences a taste of one thing and the smell of another, he goes here and there but he doesn't meet up with a damn soul and nothing happens to him, until the end when there's all that mess, and then it's over and you're left with a great confused blur in your head. All that mess comes a bit late. But at the moment I'm no judge, and even if you were Thomas Mann I don't think I'd realize it.

Yours

Lucrezia

GIUSEPPE TO ALBINA

Princeton, 30th May

Dear Albina,

I heard from Roberta that you are married, and I send you my best wishes, I'm very happy for you. Roberta often phones me and gives me news of everyone, Lucrezia, Egisto, Serena and you, and in this way I follow you all at a distance. I hope you will be happy. I think you are someone who is made to have a house and children, even though you have that boyish look, and even though, as you keep saying, you find bed a problem.

I've never written to you since I left Italy, and you have never written to me either, though you promised me you would write and I promised I'd write to you. But I always remember you, I see you sitting at the table at Mariuccia's, when we used to eat together, and then at Monte Fermo when you played the flute, I see your long, thin hands, like a lizard's as Lucrezia used to say, your chestnut-brown eyes, and your curls falling forward over your forehead. I don't know anything about your husband, whether he's young or old, Roberta didn't know and on long distance 'phone calls the money is ticking away and there isn't time to say much. I got married too, a year-and-a-half ago, as you must have heard; I married my brother's widow, and I teach Italian literature in a school. I've written a novel, which I sent to Lucrezia, but Lucrezia is going through a difficult time and so she read it rather half-heartedly and she says she feels unable to judge it. I understand, and I'm not offended. Go and see her if you happen to be in Rome, I think she needs friends, above all old, loyal friends who'll help her to regain her former spirits. She has broken up her marriage and had a baby who died immediately, she's alone, and I read her letters and wish I could be there with her, but I can't come at the moment for various reasons. My wife's daughter left her husband a few months ago and is staying with us with her baby girl, and there is some tension in the house, my wife and her daughter don't get on very well and my presence is useful because if I were not here these two women would row openly, and then I'm very busy with the baby and I take her out for walks; neither my wife nor my step-daughter can be bothered to spend time with her. The little girl is two now; she is called Maggie, and she's a delicious little creature.

With love from

Giuseppe

LUCREZIA TO GIUSEPPE

Rome, 5th June

Zezé is black, fat, with big hips, thin shoulders and legs, and large, bony, flat feet. She is about as tall as I am and she tells me I'm the tallest lady she's worked for. She arrives at midday with bags full of shopping. When it rains she has a fake tiger-skin raincoat. When she does the housework she puts a handkerchief on her head, like a turban. She was born in Capo Verde, but grew up in an aunt's house in Torpignattara.

She doesn't like tall women. She is tall but well proportioned. Luckily she has slim legs, it's a pity that my legs are not very slim. I have small breasts and hers are large, and if a woman is tall she should have large breasts otherwise she looks like a tree-trunk with a couple of bumps on it. She thinks I do my hair badly. If I have my hair all gathered up on top of my head like that it makes my face look too thin and it shows the circles round my eyes and the wrinkles. She has a full face and there's no need for her to hide it with her hair. Her hair is tight, curly and thick. She cuts it very short and she just has to ruffle it over her forehead a bit for it to look nice. Luckily her hair is still black. But I have lots of white hairs and goodness only knows why I don't dye them.

At the moment I am the only lady she works for. Before she comes to me she goes to piazza San Cosimato: she has an hour at Egisto's where there's nothing to do because Egisto is clean and tidy, and then two hours on the floor below at Alberico's, and there it's a real mess. There are no ladies at Egisto's or at Alberico's. There is Nadia at Alberico's, but you couldn't call her a lady. She comes from a rich family but she's a whore. Anyway she doesn't give orders and she doesn't give a tinker's curse about anything. Alberico gives the orders. After she's been at my house she goes to do the ironing at an architect's, and there aren't any ladies there either. She likes working when there's at least one lady there.

She comes to my house at midday and leaves at a quarter past four. She is supposed to go and pick Vito up from his kindergarten at four, but she doesn't like to. Vito is too lively and she doesn't want to run along the street after him. She doesn't like taking children for walks. Though she takes Giorgina, Alberico's baby, with her sometimes when she goes shopping, just to get her out of that mess for a moment or two. She is a very intelligent child, much more intelligent than Vito who is three years older. She's a little love that baby is, one day she'll bring her for me to see. Alberico adores that baby. Though Alberico isn't her father, no one's set eyes on her father. Alberico gave her his name out of pity. And the baby adores Alberico too, she calls him Tico. If Tico goes out she cries. She'll only eat when he's there. But that baby never wants to eat, and anyway they give her such unsuitable things, tagliatelle and sauce first thing in the morning, mussels in brine, never a cup of milk, once Zezé tried to give her a cup of bread and milk but she wasn't used to it, she asked for her tagliatelle again, but she didn't want it really and she picked the tagliatelle strands up and stuck them on the wall one by one. She doesn't want to eat with her mother. And anyway her mother doesn't give a tinker's curse about the baby or about anything. She's a little whore. She often spends the night out somewhere, comes back dead tired the next morning and throws herself down and sleeps and no one bothers her for a while. When Zezé is ready to go the little whore wakes up and asks for coffee. Salvatore yells at her to get up and get it herself. Fucking queen, she yells back and then he comes and drags her out of bed and they start brawling. Salvatore's terrifying when he loses his temper and once he nearly strangled her, Alberico tore his hands away just in time. They're all a bunch of queers there and so you can understand that she spends the night outside, with men who aren't queers, but Zezé thinks that she gets a lot of money doing it and hides the money somewhere, and when she and Salvatore row the real reason is the money because she doesn't want to tell him where she's hidden it, or the drugs she doesn't want to tell him where she's hidden, because they're all on drugs, Zezé's certain of that, she's seen the syringes. Sometimes Salvatore spends the night out too and Alberico stays alone in the house with the baby. What a mess. Boys who come and go, all queers, Adelmo, Luciano, Gianni, Zezé knows them all. They are nice to her and sweet with the baby, they're not bad people. Salvatore isn't bad either, but he has an ugly character, he argues with everyone and when he argues he's like an animal. He argues with Alberico even, but never very violently, Zezé has never seen him brawling with Alberico. When Zezé arrives she has to start washing the dishes, and there are always lots of them, unless they've had lunch sent up from a restaurant, and then all she has to do is put the dirty dishes in a basket and take them back. Zezé suggested they use paper plates when they make lunch themselves, but Alberico didn't want to know anything about paper plates, they make him melancholy. Once Salvatore used to wash the dishes but now he's fed up because there are always so many people eating there – Adelmo, Luca, Gianni, Giuliano often stay and eat with them. It's Alberico who decides whether they get lunch sent up from a restaurant or cook for themselves. He is in charge, and anyway he has the money. He's the one who wants Zezé to come every day, and he's the one who pays her at the end of the week. He's very rich and he'll be even richer because in a few days they're showing his film. He always types in the kitchen, naked except for red underpants, with oropax in his ears, sometimes with the baby on his knee. Every now and then they give supper parties for fifteen people and then they ask Zezé to cook. Zezé makes them bowls of pasta and bowls of mixed salad, lettuce, cucumbers and peppers, never meat because they don't eat meat, it's corpses Alberico says. Zezé pointed out that fish are corpses too, sardines, mussels, squid, all of which they buy often enough. But Alberico thinks that meat more than anything else gives the feeling of being a corpse because when you buy it and eat it you think of hair and blood, but when you eat fish you don't think of these things, fish don't have hair and their blood is different, colder and clearer. Egisto is usually at these supper parties and also 'I', the doctor as Zezé called him when she used to see him here, now she calls him Fegisse, doctor Fegisse, and usually doctor Fegisse brings along that little thin thing with the nose. She's someone who doesn't eat anything. She just wants a stick of celery and a cup of hot water. Once she asked for a carrot but there weren't any carrots in the house.

She's called Ippo. She's an ugly little thing, Ippo, but Fegisse prefers her to me because she dresses well and has really beautiful hair, thick, tight and curly à la Angela Davis, and besides she's quite small and small women are always very lucky. When it's half past four Zezé takes the handkerchief off her head and her black, tight, thick hair à la Angela Davis appears, which is even more beautiful than Ippo's because it's black. She goes off to the architect's. She has put a lot of money aside and soon she will buy a flat. She wants it to be in old Rome. Where I am is old Rome too, but she prefers the area around the Pantheon.

Yours

Lucrezia

GIUSEPPE TO ALBERICO

Princeton, 25th June

Dear Alberico,

Roberta phoned me and told me that your film will have its première in a few days. I send you my best wishes and hope that it will be a success.

I've heard about you from other people too. I know that you're very busy and that your house is always full of people. I know that you often eat squid and mussels in brine, I know that you type naked, except for red underpants, with oropax in your ears and the baby on your knee. I see you like that, and it's a reassuring picture. I'm very pleased that you are working. You use a typewriter when you write, I write in long-hand as you know. I have written a novel. It is called *The Knot.* Naturally I'd be pleased if you read it. I've sent it to Lucrezia and perhaps you could ask her to let you have a look at it. I don't know if you'd like to. Two agencies have already turned it down. Nevertheless I haven't given up the idea of having it published. A friend of mine, someone called Danny, is thinking of sending it to a third agency.

This Danny is Chantal's ex-husband. Chantal is my wife's daughter, my stepdaughter. What a strange phrase stepdaughter is, I really cannot connect it with Chantal or with my relationship with her.

As we write to each other so rarely, and telephone so rarely, I feel that every now and again I have to explain who these people I talk about are. Besides, you have a bad memory, or at least you have a bad memory when it comes to the things I tell you about myself.

You and I live in very different ways. You are surrounded by people, so much so that when you are at home you have to put oropax in your ears. You always eat with lots of people and you give supper parties. I never see anyone except the students who take my course, and Danny when he comes to Princeton to see his little girl, and our neighbour Mrs Mortimer, and in the evenings Schultz and Kramer who were friends of my brother. I don't see anyone else. Anne Marie, Chantal and I are alone a great deal. Sometimes I am afraid that Chantal is bored and I try to make her go out. Over the last few weeks she has got to know a group of students and she goes out with them in the evenings. I'm pleased about this. I bath the baby, give her her supper and put her to bed. Anne Marie has no patience with children. When I was young I didn't have much patience with children, but I've changed as I've grown older.

I was pleased to hear from Roberta that you are still going to Dr Lanzara for psychoanalysis. I ought to say that I'm especially pleased because Dr Lanzara is living in my house. That house is still mine and it always will be. A man can sell his house or give it to someone else to his heart's content, but he always keeps it within himself nevertheless. I find it reassuring that for a few hours of the day you are between those walls. I don't, to tell you the truth, set much store by psychoanalysis. Whilst I've been going through a difficult patch I've been tempted to go to an analyst, but I've immediately rejected the idea. On the other hand it's possible that talking to Dr Lanzara is very useful to you. Remember me to both the Lanzaras, husband and wife, and remember me to the walls of my house.

The other news I hear about you is less reassuring. I haven't heard it from Roberta, but from other sources, and I hope it's not true. Roberta says it's not true. She says that you have a fundamentally healthy character and a core of deep common sense. I'd like to believe that this is so.

I think I might be able to come to Italy next autumn. I'll come with Anne Marie and Chantal. And so you will meet the people I love and with whom I spend my life. I thought you would come to see me in America, but I see that you have too much to do in Italy.

With love from

your father

ALBERICO TO GIUSEPPE

Rome, 4th July

Respected father,

My film's première was yesterday evening. I didn't go. People tell me it was well-received. I don't like it at all. I enjoyed myself making it, but I don't like it. However, if other people like it, so much the better.

A lady who comes and cleans for me has brought me your novel. I telephoned that friend of yours, Lucrezia, to ask her to let me have it. The lady who comes to my flat also goes to hers. And so this morning she left it on the table for me, and I will read it.

The things people tell you about me are often wrong. I don't put oropax in my ears. My underpants are not red but black.

With love from

Alberico

I've just realized that the last phrase in my letter could be misinterpreted. In fact the colour of my underpants has no special significance. I don't like black. I buy black underpants so that I won't have to wash them so often.

ROBERTA TO GIUSEPPE

Rome, 4th July

Dear Giuseppe,

Yesterday evening Alberico's film *Deviance* was shown. It was shown in a little private hall on via Flaminia. It was a great success. There were lots of people. Alberico wasn't there. I phoned him and he said he hadn't come because he had a headache. Nadia, Salvatore, Adelmo – all the friends I meet when I go to see him – were there. Nadia had a little, round, black straw hat perched on top of her head.

The film was lovely. It is well-directed. It all happens in a big restored farmhouse in the country. The rooms are large and half-empty with white curtains fluttering about, and tiled floors. There's a constant bright white light. I shan't tell you the plot, mainly because I couldn't follow all of it, there was something wrong with the soundtrack and I was sitting in the last row at the back. There is a boy, a girl and an old man. Then guests come. There are some drugs hidden in the farmhouse but no one knows where. It's an upsetting film because the white light is there the whole time, and because little by little everyone dies. But the most upsetting thing is the light, the white walls, the tiled floors and the fluttering curtains. Alberico told me that it cost very little to make because the farmhouse belongs to Adelmo's father and he let them have it for a small sum. The actors were amateurs, taken off the streets.

I was there with Lucrezia and the Lanzaras. However Lucrezia left half-way through the second half. She said she couldn't stand that kind of film. She was bored to death and wanted to sleep. But in fact as we went in we saw Ignazio Fegiz with his friend Ippo. They were sitting in the front row, next to Salvatore. As I told you, it's all over between Lucrezia and Ignazio Fegiz.

Lucrezia isn't well. She is run-down and is always very pale. She never recovered after the birth and loss of her baby. On top of which 'I' has left her. She must think that she has destroyed her marriage for nothing, for a relationship with someone who has other relationships that are clearly more binding. I often go to her house but I don't know if she likes seeing me. She is always saying she likes to be alone. If you've gone all the way across the city to see her and keep her company for a while, you feel put out. She says that Rome is a hateful city inhabited by hateful people. She wants to live in another city, she doesn't know which one. Nevertheless at the same time she says she needs a house in Rome. In a few months time she will have to leave the one she is in. I tell her that a psychoanalyst might help. She gets annoyed. She doesn't believe in psychoanalysis. She doesn't like psychoanalysts. She doesn't like Dr Lanzara. She thinks it's a crazy idea having that bald head in front of her and having to tell him about herself. I tell her she could go to a different one. But a different one would have some other unbearable characteristic. And anyway psychoanalysts cost money and she has very little money. I try to point out that she doesn't have so little. She is very open with me and I know how much she has. Not that little but when someone gets it into her head that she doesn't have much money, it's difficult to convince her that it's not true. You were the same when you went to America, you'd got it into your head that you didn't know how you could manage here. You remember how I tried to point out to you that you did have money and that you would be able to get by very well indeed? You left, and I don't know whether you did well or you did badly to move to America. Perhaps you did well seeing that you've got married and settled down.

A few evenings ago, *Mirra* had its opening night in a very small inconvenient theatre, a long way away, on via Olimpia. Serena was acting in it. You know that to act in *Mirra* was always the great dream of her life. Lucrezia and I went. Serena's father was there, he'd come down from Genoa. He sat in the front row, with his great white moustache. Albina was there, she had come specially from Luco dei Marsi. Egisto was there. It was a modern dress *Mirra*. Serena was wearing black slacks and a jumper. The stage was empty, there was just a little iron ladder. There wasn't much applause and the newspapers the next day tore it to pieces.

Nevertheless, Lucrezia told me that Serena was very happy. She seemed happy on the evening of the first night too, when we went to see her in her dressing-room, and she wasn't at all aware that there had been so little applause. She was going to have supper in a pizzeria near the theatre, with the director and the other actors, and she asked if we would like to go with them, but it was perfectly clear that she wanted us to disappear. Her father was tired, he took a taxi and went back to his hotel. We – Lucrezia, Albina, Egisto and I – went to a pizzeria a little further away, but after a while we saw Serena and her group arrive, perhaps because the other pizzeria was closed. Serena made great hello-there gestures but didn't come over to us, she sat with her group at a table at the end of the room. Egisto remarked that she was very rude, and that she should have invited us to sit at her table. But Albina said that she could understand her, that she was in her new surroundings, and that she didn't want to see our old faces around her. So we tried to chat among ourselves and not to look at the other table. Egisto and Albina started to talk about the Women's Centre in Pianura, when Serena acted Gemma Donati, but all of a sudden Lucrezia said that she was tired and felt sleepy, she got up and left, going straight between the tables without turning round. We thought that she was offended by Serena's behaviour, and Serena must have thought so too, because I saw her glance towards the door. Lucrezia told me later that she couldn't care less about Serena's rudeness, but that she had suddenly felt very sad when she remembered Pianura, the Women's Centre, Monte Fermo, those places, those people, those years. Albina went to sleep at Egisto's because Serena lives in her bedsit now, perhaps with her director, who is called Umberto and with whom she is very happy.

Albina, as you know, is married, but her life is the same as before, except that now she has to cook for her husband as well, and iron her husband's shirts as well as her brother's and father's.

Alberico's film had very favourable reviews. I will send you the cuttings. I phoned to congratulate him, but he said that they were all idiotic. He is already working on another film.

With love from

Roberta

LUCREZIA TO GIUSEPPE

Rome, 10th July

I went to see your son's film. I thought it was really awful. However, I was the only person who thought it was really awful. Everyone else praised it to the skies.

'I' was there with Ippo. So I've finally seen her. I've seen the famous hair.

I also went to *Mirra*. I can't remember whether I've told you that Serena has finally been able to say 'Now I am dying, Empia' in a theatre. Now she says it every evening. She has a man, and she's very happy. She hardly ever phones me.

I saw Albina. She came to Rome to see *Mirra*. She came alone, in her station-wagon. She has got her licence and bought a second-hand station-wagon. She uses it for going around the countryside looking for timber. Her husband has a furniture factory. To look at she's just the same, with her dry lizard's claws, and her handbag that's always open with kleenex and biscuits spilling out of it. But inside she has changed. It's as if she has become dry inside too, serious and hard. She and I no longer had anything to say to each other. I asked her if bed were still a problem for her. She didn't smile, she remained serious. She said no and quickly changed the subject. I think it's a very big problem for her.

Yours

Lucrezia

EGISTO TO GIUSEPPE

Rome, 20th July

Dear Giuseppe,

Roberta told me she would phone you. But I don't know if she has or not. Something terrible has happened. Nadia is dead.

It happened five days ago. Nadia, Salvatore and Adelmo went to the cinema. Alberico stayed at home and two of his friends who are always there were with him, Giuliano and Gianni. It was around midnight when Adelmo phoned. He was phoning from the General Hospital. Nadia was in the emergency ward and she was dying.

What I know I learnt from Adelmo. But Adelmo remembers everything in a very confused way. They came out of the cinema. They had bought an ice-cream from a kiosk. They were walking towards the car which was parked in piazza Tuscolo. Two men appeared on a scooter. They were a couple of kids, Adelmo says, they must have been seventeen or eighteen. They came up to Salvatore and said they wanted a word with him. And then four others got out of a Fiat 500 that was parked on the corner. One of them had a long blond pony-tail. They all went for Salvatore together and started beating him up. Nadia threw herself into the middle of it all and yelled out for them to leave him alone. Salvatore's jumper was torn and one hand was bleeding. Nadia got in front of him. One of them opened fire. Adelmo thought it was the one with the pony-tail but he isn't sure. They wanted to shoot Salvatore but it was Nadia who fell. People came. Someone called the emergency services. All of a sudden Adelmo could see neither Salvatore nor the two on the scooter nor the others. He thought he could still see the pony-tail for a moment. Nadia was lying on the ground. An ambulance arrived and immediately afterwards two police jeeps.

Alberico called me. We took my car and went to the General Hospital, to the emergency. Gianni stayed in the flat with the baby.

Nadia was already dead. Her clothes were in a corner on the floor, her jeans, her underclothes, a sweatshirt stained with blood. *Pepsicola* was written across the sweatshirt, just where the bullet hole was. Her sweatshirts always had something written on them.

Alberico wanted to pick up the clothes. But a sister told him that he must not touch them because the police would need them. She told him to go home and bring some other clothes. She asked him if he were her brother or husband or her companion or what. Her companion he answered.

I went to the house to get some other clothes. Gianni and I started looking for something suitable. But there wasn't much to choose from. Her clothes were all just rags. I finally found a blouse and a long skirt.

Alberico was questioned by the police. Adelmo was questioned too, at great length, and they kept him in. But the parking-lot attendant said he wasn't one of those who were doing the beating up. Adelmo came out yesterday.

This morning the police came to search the apartment. They turned everything upside down but they didn't find anything. Afterwards Alberico and I and Zezé, the woman who comes to do the cleaning, had to put everything back again.

Over these past few days I have been with Alberico a lot. I asked him if he knew who the two on the scooter and the others in the Fiat 500 were. He told me he didn't know anything about it, and I believe him. Salvatore was very close, and he never told anyone anything about himself. Sometimes he spent the night away from the house. Sometimes he used to disappear for a week and not say a word to anyone. When he came back he didn't say where he'd been, but he'd have a bag full of eggs and sausages and perhaps he'd been to his mother's, in Frosinone. We realized we were talking about Salvatore in the past tense, as if he too were dead, or had disappeared for good.

Roberta telephoned Nadia's parents. Her father arrived with a cousin. The mother hadn't come because she has a heart disease.

Nadia's name was Nadia Alba Desiderata Astarita. Her father's name is Altiero Astarita. He is a little old man with a small bristly grey beard. There was a mass said in the chapel at the hospital. All Alberico's friends were there. Zezé was there and also Ignazio Fegiz with Ippo. Nadia was taken back to Catania, where there is a family tomb.

Altiero Astarita told Roberta that he would begin civil proceedings against persons unknown.

He kept telling Roberta that he would come and take the child. Alberico told Roberta that he didn't want to give her to him. She was legally his child, and he could decide what to do about her.

Alberico couldn't sleep at night and I stayed with him till late. He kept thinking the same thing, that if he had also gone to the cinema that night, if he had been there in piazza Tuscolo, Nadia would not be dead. He would have held her back, away from all the fighting. He could have left the baby at home with Gianni, or taken her along with them as they had done so many times when they had all wanted to go to the cinema.

Alberico says that now, without Nadia and without Salvatore, the house seems empty. Though it's not empty, there's still the usual coming and going. Alberico has packed all of Nadia's clothes into two parcels and is sending them to Sicily. But they were just rags. The baby found one of her hats – a hard round hat made of straw – and she puts it on her head and wanders through the rooms with this hat on that comes down as far as her mouth. Zezé and Gianni are arguing about her magazines, she had thousands of them.

Giuseppe, I've heard that you had half a mind to come over, and now is the right moment, so come. Alberico is going through a difficult time, and there is the risk that they will try and take the child away from him; perhaps you could be of some help to him, I don't know.

Egisto

EGISTO TO GIUSEPPE

Rome, 2nd August

Dear Giuseppe,

I'll continue from where I left off in the letter I wrote to you ten days ago. I haven't had any reply. I know that you have phoned Roberta for news.

Nadia's father, Altiero Astarita, came back here, talked to Alberico for a whole afternoon, collected the child and took her off to Sicily. I was there when he talked to Alberico, because Alberico wanted me to be present.

Altiero Astarita said that he would leave for Sicily immediately with the baby, and he begged Alberico not to oppose him, otherwise he would refer the case to the courts. And then a long drawn-out legal dispute would be initiated and this would be sad and humiliating for everyone. The child would do well in Sicily. He and his wife live in the country, in a village called Acquedolci near Catania. They have a big house there and many hectares of land laid out as orchards. The child would have fresh air, fresh fruit, fresh eggs and she would grow up healthy. If Alberico wished to see her he could come and stay at their house in Acquedolci for a while and he would be made extremely welcome. He and his wife knew that he was not the child's real father and that he had given her his name because of a generous and noble impulse, which they greatly appreciated. They were also ready to give him some money to compensate him for all the expenses he had incurred. Alberico stayed silent. He was sitting at the table, doodling on a sheet of paper.

Altiero Astarita turned towards me and continued talking. Here in Rome, he said, the child was not doing well. The apartment was not a suitable place for a child. It was quite chaotic. It was in fact, to be quite clear about it, a real shambles. The courts would never consent to allow the child to remain here, in such a shambles. Then Alberico screwed up the sheet of paper he had been scribbling on; he stood up and said he had had enough. He was tired. He didn't want money, it wasn't of any use to him, and if he started to talk about money again he would grab him by the jacket and throw him downstairs. Altiero Astarita said he could not put up with such language. Alberico said he couldn't put up with his face. If he would please leave immediately. Please. Altiero Astarita left.

He came back the next morning and he had two suitcases and his cousin with him. He also had a strapping girl of about fourteen with him; she was slow and sullen, the daughter of a labourer in Acquedolci, and she had been brought along to look after the child on the way back. I was on the floor below, because Zezé had phoned me when she saw them arriving. Altiero Astarita told me that their train left at midday. He preferred trains to aeroplanes. He told me that he was pleased to see me because I seemed to him to be the one person in all that shambles who had his head screwed on properly.

Alberico was in his room typing. Renato and Gianni were with him. He said to me that if that bearded little shit wanted to take the child, let him take her. He didn't want to fight about it. And besides, perhaps it was true that the child would be better off in Sicily than with him. Happier, perhaps. He didn't want to see the child again and he would never go to Sicily to see her, never. He didn't want to see her whilst they were taking her away. He didn't want to say goodbye to her. He had always hated goodbyes, he hated them.

Altiero Astarita ordered the cousin and the labourer's daughter to put the child's clothes and toys in a suitcase. The child didn't have many clothes, and she didn't have any toys, or rather she had just one, a three-foot-high inflatable penguin that squawked when you squeezed its belly – Salvatore had won it on a shooting-range. Usually the child didn't even look at it, but that morning she did nothing but squeeze its belly and listen to it squawk. The labourer's daughter wanted to deflate it and put it in the suitcase, but the child wouldn't let her touch it. Altiero Astarita was in a hurry, but there were various hold-ups, jumpers that had been washed and were not dry, the penguin, the child who didn't want to be washed, the labourer's daughter who went around looking for a plaster because she had a blister on her foot. Alberico never left his room. They finally called a taxi and left, the child crying in the cousin's arms, the labourer's daughter carrying the two half-empty suitcases, Altiero Astarita in an irritable state. The penguin was left in the hall, half-deflated, and later Gianni took it away.

Salvatore was discovered in Frosinone, in his mother's house. They kept him in jail for two days, then they let him out. Adelmo went to his house. He said he was sitting in the kitchen near the window, with a bandage round one hand, and that he didn't say a word. His hand had been wounded with a penknife that evening, and it didn't get better because it was infected. Adelmo stayed there for a while but was unable to get a single syllable out of him. His mother said that he was always like that now, silent, motionless, with those staring eyes. His mother is an elementary school teacher.

Yours

Egisto

GIUSEPPE TO ALBERICO

Princeton, 15th August

Dear Alberico,

I have heard what has happened from Roberta and from Egisto. Egisto especially has given me a very detailed account. Roberta often phones me, and she says she often goes to your flat to see you. She says that you have stopped going to Dr Lanzara's. I'm sorry about this because I think you should be going there, as you are passing through such a difficult and sad time.

I only saw Nadia once, that day in Florence. Roberta and Ignazio Fegiz were there, and the friend you had then, a German, I think he was called Rainer. I remember Nadia was short and seemed like a child. She was wearing blue overalls with braces. I remember, she had a tiny face and short fluffy hair à la Angela Davis. I think I wondered for a moment if she could be, or could become, your girl-friend. It was a stupid thought and I quickly erased it from my mind and inwardly asked your pardon. I've always found it difficult to accept the fact that you are not attracted to women, because people want their sons to be like themselves. But basically I have accepted this fact, in the same way that I have accepted other things about you and your life which were not easy for me to either understand or accept.

You used to tell me that Nadia was a stupid girl. Nevertheless you lived with her for a long time, and you must have felt, in some way or other, attached to her. It must be painful for you to have lost her, and to have lost her in such horrifying circumstances. But her death was a fine one – proud, brave and noble. She died saving someone else's life.

It must be extremely painful for you now that they have taken the child from you. But then I think it wouldn't have been easy for you to bring up a little child that had lost her mother.

I am coming, I am certainly coming, but not straightaway. Something has happened to me too, not a disaster perhaps but something that I find upsetting at the moment. My step-daughter Chantal has walked out of the house unexpectedly, and for some days we had no news, and then she wrote to us from New York. She has left her child Maggie here, and I look after her because Anne Marie has neither the time nor the patience to concern herself with her. Because of this I can't leave the house at the moment. Anne Marie is worried and upset. Chantal left late in the evening without saying anything; she took a little travelling bag with her creams and pyjamas in. We thought she was at the cinema, then we found her note in the kitchen under the scales. She didn't give an address. She simply said that someone had mentioned a job to her in New York and that she had gone. She would come and collect the child later.

After some days we heard from a friend of hers that she was living in a commune and that she was working as a waitress in a restaurant. Here she was working in a tourist agency and she had an excellent job. She finally phoned us the day before yesterday. I answered the phone. But she said very little. She said she didn't want to see either me or her mother. She wanted to be left in peace. She laughed in a shrill, drawn-out, nervous way. Chantal has these sudden shrill bursts of laughter – there is nothing happy about them – that stay ringing in your ears for a long time.

I've finished up by talking about me, or rather about Chantal and the things that have been happening here. And really I just wanted to talk about you. I heard from Roberta that your film is doing well, and that lots of people go and see it. I'm pleased that it has been such a success for you.

With love from

your father

ALBERICO TO GIUSEPPE

Rome, 3rd September

Dear father,

Thank you for your letter.

Yes, as Roberta told you, I've stopped the course of psychoanalysis. But I'm still friends with the Lanzaras and I see them now and again. They are nice people. I have an ice-cream with them sometimes in the evenings, at the Café Esperia, which I think you know well. It's the café on the corner of via Nazario Sauro and via Maroncelli. I don't know if you remember it. I don't know what you can remember and what you can't, you've been away for so long.

Dr Lanzara insists that I start the psychoanalysis again, but at the moment I don't want to. But I don't mind sitting with him in the Café Esperia. I have his bald, dry head in front of me, as smooth as an egg. I eat my ice-cream, watch the people going by and breathe in the fresh evening air. I feel fine, much better than in his consulting room. I like his head, it's familiar to me. In his consulting room I feel obliged to talk, but like this I can stay silent too.

The Lanzaras are selling their flat. They are thinking of going to live in England again, where they lived for years. I thought of buying it myself and I suggested it to them, but it seems that it's not right for a psychoanalyst to sell his house to one of his ex-patients. Why this shouldn't be right I don't begin to understand. However this is an obstacle that can be overcome. For example, you could buy it and give it to me. I would give you the money to do this. I am well-off at the moment because I have earned a lot from my film. This house would be, Roberta says, an excellent investment. She says that bricks and mortar never let you down. It's true that I would pay much more than double what you got for it. First, because the price of houses has gone up enormously, and second because the Lanzaras are good at business. Roberta says that you and I do not resemble each other in anything, but we do resemble each other in our readiness to be taken in by outright swindles. She used to say that I was sly about money but now she says the opposite. She says that now she understands me better and she has realized that actually money means nothing to me. And in fact this is true.

I think I'd enjoy living in that house. I don't know, I know that I have come to hate the apartment I live in at the moment. I hate every corner of it, every bit of wall. I'm not alone here because there's always some friend or other of mine sleeping here. But I really want to change where I live. I'm seriously thinking of buying your old home in via Nazario Sauro.

Yes, they took the child. I let them do it because I thought it was better for her. She will grow up in the country. She will have fresh air, chickens, fresh eggs. Not that I think the country and fresh eggs are everything. But they are a lot. And I didn't feel certain that I would be able to give her anything more essential.

The fact of her now being without a mother has not actually changed that much for the child. Nadia wasn't much of a mother; as such she more or less didn't exist. It was always me who looked after the child. But I said that she *more or less* didn't exist as a mother, and that *more or less* could be extremely important. I don't know. In any case Nadia's parents said that with them the child would have a better life. It's possible that what they said was true. I don't know. The old man who came to collect her wasn't unpleasant. I hated him and would have gladly strangled him, but I must say that I didn't find him wholly unpleasant. Anyway, they took the child away and now I want to stop thinking about it.

I haven't read your novel yet. Too many things have happened to me recently. It's still there on the table in its sky-blue cover. I will read it as soon as I can. I'm not a great novel reader. I never have been. At the moment I don't read anything. I don't even read the newspapers.

You mention Ignazio Fegiz in your letter. I see him quite often. I see him with that friend of his, Ippo. Sometimes we meet in the evenings in a restaurant in piazza Navona. Egisto and I, my neighbour from upstairs, sit at a table and wait for them. We see them arrive slowly, he is tall and upright with a crew-cut, and she is small, leaning forward a little, all nose. Egisto calls them the Cat and the Fox. He, Ignazio Fegiz, had an affair with that other friend of yours, Lucrezia, but it was an affair that came to an abrupt conclusion. He doesn't know how to get away from Ippo. To tell you the truth I can't stand Ippo. She's really neurotic. She only eats carrots. I get on quite well with Ignazio Fegiz and with Egisto. Perhaps because I'm always with young people and so every now and then I want to see someone older. And I'll be getting old too. This is a time in which people get old quickly. It's a time in which everything happens quickly.

I know that my neighbour Egisto has told you to come here. Don't take any notice, it's not necessary that you come. Even he thinks I need company. In fact I don't need anything. I've more company that I know what to do with. I'm never alone.

That friend of mine, Salvatore Ostuni, tried to hang himself in his mother's house at Frosinone. His mother was out and she arrived just in time, if she had come a moment later it would have been all over. He's in a mental hospital now.

No one knows what happened in piazza Tuscolo that evening. Salvatore doesn't speak and when he does speak he doesn't say even a syllable that's true. He says that the two on the scooter wanted a gold watch back from him and that he didn't want to give it to them because they hadn't given him a sum of money – three million – that he'd lent them. The ones in the Fiat 500 were friends of the ones on the scooter. He didn't see who it was who shot at him, he can't remember, he doesn't know.

Alberico

LUCREZIA TO GIUSEPPE

Rome, 5th October

Dear Giuseppe,

I haven't written to you for a long time, and you haven't written to me any more either.

I heard about Nadia. I can't stop thinking about it. I saw her twice in all. Once at Monte Fermo. Once at your son's film, that awful film. I only looked vaguely at her each time, and I can't remember her well. Goodness knows why we look at people so vaguely. Then they die and we wish we were able to remember them.

I spent August and September at Sabaudia, with Daniele and Vito, in a house that Serena has rented for the whole year. The others went to a summer camp, and then they went to Holland with Piero. I was very alone at Sabaudia, Serena didn't come at all. It was a quiet summer.

Write to me.

Lucrezia

GIUSEPPE TO LUCREZIA

Princeton, 15th October

Dear Lucrezia,

It's true we haven't written to each other for quite a while.

I think about Nadia all the time too. I only saw her once. In Florence. I feel as if a century has gone by since that day.

I'm going through a difficult time at the moment. This is why I haven't written to you.

In my letter I've often talked about Chantal. I don't know if you realized what was happening to me. I don't know if you realized that I had fallen in love with Chantal.

I didn't notice it immediately. Or perhaps I pretended not to notice it. I hid it from myself. But I'm sure you noticed it immediately, and I'm sure Anne Marie did too.

Relations between mother and daughter were already bad, and little by little they became impossible.

Now Chantal is in New York. She works in a restaurant. The child has remained with us. Anne Marie doesn't look after her, she says she hasn't time. It's me who looks after the child.

A few days ago I went to New York. I left the child with Mrs Mortimer.

I stayed at the Continental Hotel on Fifth Avenue. The few times that I've happened to be in New York I've always stayed at that hotel.

I went to the restaurant where Chantal works. She was carrying a tray and was in a hurry, she said she would phone me that evening at the hotel. I waited the whole evening for her to call me. She didn't call. It was a hellish evening. I drank a lot of whisky while I was waiting. I tell you I drink a lot these days.

The next day I went to the restaurant. I sat at a table and ordered a hamburger and a beer. After a while Chantal came and sat opposite me. She said that she was grateful to me for looking after the child. She said she would soon come to Princeton to collect her. As soon as she had a room to herself, because at the moment she was living in a commune. She gave one of her shrill, drawn-out bursts of laughter, like a bird's shriek. Chantal laughs a lot, for no reason. I laughed with her too, joylessly, in humiliation and despair. The hamburger was on my plate; I couldn't eat it. Then she suddenly became serious and told me to leave immediately. I left.

She and I made love only once, in the room with the bear-cubs.

Anne Marie had gone to a party at the house of some colleagues of hers from the Institute. The child was with Mrs Mortimer.

Then the telephone rang. I answered. It was Anne Marie and she said she would be a little late. Chantal went to have a shower. I went to fetch the child. I happened to stay at Mrs Mortimer's for a while because she wanted to show me some photographs. When I returned Anne Marie had returned too, she was sitting in the living-room examining her white spangled shawl which she always wore to parties and on which there was a little coffee stain. She and Chantal were discussing how to get the stain out.

I don't know if Anne Marie sensed something strange in my voice when I answered the phone, or if she saw something strange in my face, or in her daughter's face, when she returned to the house. I know that that evening at supper she talked at great length about the party, who was there and who wasn't. I watched Chantal; she was calm. Chantal left a few days later. She and I had not exchanged a single word since that evening.

For the first few days after Chantal left Anne Marie was very distressed and in the evenings she sat by the telephone and waited for Chantal to get in touch. Then as soon as she heard where she was she reassumed her calm exterior. Just that now and again while she and I were talking about something ordinary and banal red blotches would suddenly appear on her neck and her mouth would turn down and tremble. Now I try to make her think of the child. Anne Marie and the child don't like each other at all, however she feels ashamed and sorry that she doesn't like her and for a moment feels that she ought to look at her and smile at her. The child's presence makes our situation a little more bearable, a little easier.

Anne Marie said that the child could not sleep on the ground floor alone. One of us would have to sleep near her. I moved down to the ground floor, into a long, narrow room where our suitcases are piled up. The room with the bear-cubs, where the baby sleeps, is next door. And so if the baby wakes at night I hear her immediately.

Danny came yesterday. I was pleased to see him because he is really the only friend I have here. It's true that I never tell him anything about myself now, but I get great pleasure out of seeing him. As usual, I visited him, with the child, in that squalid rooming-house he stays in. We talked for a long time, as usual. We drank whisky. Then we went for a walk with the child in the park. We talked about the child, about Anne Marie, about the Pippolos, about Chantal's character. I don't know if he realized what had happened. Danny is a dear boy, but not very quick on the uptake, and above all far too involved in his own personal problems. He asked me to lend him some money again, and I did so. He has to send money to the Pippolos, who desperately need it. He thanked me for looking after the child. Just at the moment it was impossible for him to take her away. He gave me back a copy of the English translation of my novel, which he still had with him. He had read it and thought it interesting, but written in a very old-fashioned style. That friend of his had told him that a good three agencies had turned it down now. But I don't care about the novel any more. When I got home, I threw the copy into the bottom of the wardrobe where all the others are.

Giuseppe

EGISTO TO GIUSEPPE

Rome, 10th November

Dear Giuseppe,

I've started to read your novel. Alberico gave it to me. He doesn't have time to read it now. He has a new film in his head and he doesn't read anything. Not even the newspapers.

I hope you won't mind that he has given it to me. I've read about twenty pages. It's good. A bit stiff. But good.

Yesterday evening I was with Alberico and I suggested to him that we go and see Lucrezia. He didn't want to. But I persuaded him. When we arrived Lucrezia was alone. She is alone a great deal. You remember how once she used to be surrounded by people. *Le Margherite* was like a sea-port. Now, here in Rome, she almost never sees anyone. Serena's head is full of the theatre and she only sees actors. Serena isn't acting in *Mirra* any more, she's acting that monologue of hers now, *Gemma and the Flames,* in a little theatre in Prenestino. The newspapers tore her monologue to pieces. But she doesn't mind, she acts it all the same, happily wrapped up in her sheet. They didn't let her have the big fire she wanted here either, as in Pianura. There's still just a little brazier with a few ashes in it. On some evenings the entire audience consists of three people. But she doesn't mind. She says people don't come because the Italian theatre is in a state of crisis.

We found Lucrezia learning English from records. She's got it into her head that she'll learn English properly and then look for work as a translator. She says she needs the money. All the children were already in bed, except for Cecilia who appeared for a moment. But really they aren't children any more, except for the smallest. Vito – you remember him, the one who used to be still wandering around the house late at night with a plate of soup. Now he's in the first year of junior school. The others aren't children any more. Cecilia is sixteen, she uses eye-shadow and has a boy-friend she talks to on the phone for hours.

Yesterday evening Alberico and Lucrezia got on extraordinarily well. She immediately told him that she had seen his film *Deviance* and that she thought it was really awful. I thought that he would be put out by this but on the contrary he was pleased. He said that he thought it was terrible too. They tore *Deviance* to pieces between them, a little from her side, a little from his. And so they became friends all of a sudden. They had seen each other once before, at Monte Fermo, a few years ago. Nadia was there, she was pregnant. Alberico, Nadia and Salvatore had come to *Le Margherite*. Alberico could remember *Le Margherite*, the garden, the wood, the children. Lucrezia said that she had hardly glanced at Nadia that day and she had thought about that day when she heard she was dead. Alberico quickly changed the subject, he doesn't like talking openly about Nadia. He said that he and Lucrezia had met one other time, it had been on the landing in via Nazario Sauro. She was going to Roberta's, and he to the floor above. Then he went back to saying that *Deviance* really was an awful film. They started talking nineteen to the dozen about the film and I got bored and started to read a book. Then they talked about houses. How they got from films to houses I don't know, but Lucrezia thinks about houses a lot at the moment and talks about them a lot, because she will soon have to give up the apartment she's in. The person who lent it to her is coming back to Rome in a few months. Lucrezia reads the advertisements in *Il Messaggero*, and she telephones, but the prices are out of this world. She knew about the house in via Nazario Sauro, the one that used to be yours. She knew it was on the market because Roberta had talked to her about it, she knew the Lanzaras were leaving Rome. But she said that perhaps she didn't really want to buy that house. She knew it too well. She'd been there too many times. She had even smashed ash-trays there once. She would prefer to buy a house that she didn't know and that had no memories attached to it. Alberico said that he also knew that house very well and that he had slept there a few times, when you lived there, and then he'd gone there for psychoanalysis, and that he too would prefer a house he didn't know and that had no memories attached to it, but even so houses where we've already been at other times can be reassuring in a way. He had come to hate the apartment where he was living now. He hated every corner of it and every inch of its walls. He suggested that she take it, if he left. But she said she didn't want it because it was too small, she hadn't seen it but Zezé had described it to her. In any case they both agreed on the fact that the house in via Nazario Sauro was ridiculously expensive.

Alberico talked about another apartment that was perhaps for sale, in Porta Cavalleggeri. It was tiny but it had a beautiful terrace. It was Ippo's apartment. He asked Lucrezia if she knew Ippo. Lucrezia said she didn't. Then she said that perhaps she'd seen her once. Alberico said that Ippo was unbearable. But the apartment was charming. Perhaps she would sell it. She says that she wants to go and live in Fregene. Goodness only knows whether it's true or not. Fregene is a long way from the centre of Rome, where Ippo and Ignazio Fegiz walk about in the evenings as if they were glued together. They are like the Cat and the Fox. I was watching Lucrezia and she seemed pleased and more cheerful, there was a glint in her eyes. She is used to thinking about Ippo and Ignazio Fegiz by herself and to hear them discussed openly, and so frivolously, was a comfort to her.

We were about to leave when Piero phoned. He was in Rome and asked if he could come there to sleep. After a short while he arrived. He had a key. He came in in his big coat and long red woollen scarf. He had come from Perugia and had trouble with his car, he had had to stop in the road and there had been a big downpour of rain. He was freezing cold and asked if he could have a hot shower. He came back after a while wrapped up in Daniele's dressing-gown, which was too tight and too short for him. He said that the water was barely warm, more or less cold. Lucrezia said that she only turned the water-heater on for a few hours a day, to save money. He told her that a water-heater should be kept on all the time because you spend three times as much turning it on and off. He hadn't had any supper and asked if there were any leftovers. He went to look in the kitchen and came back with a cold cutlet. We stayed to keep him company while he ate. He seemed tired. I hadn't seen him for a while and I thought he had aged. He still has his little blond baby curls and that big, full face, but his eyes were sunken and had black circles round them. He said the cutlet was good but not very tender. It must have been an old calf, not proper veal. Lucrezia said it wasn't veal or calf it was beef and that she always bought beef because it was more nutritious and cheaper. He said that beef was marvellous for everything but not for cutlets. She said she didn't want to be criticized about her food, it was something she wouldn't put up with. We left, and in the street I thought that it is very difficult to dissolve a marriage, there are always scattered bits of it lying about and every now and again they give a twitch and draw blood.

Alberico went back to Lucrezia's today to take her some records. I am very pleased that they have become friends. I am very pleased for him and for her.

Yours

Egisto

GIUSEPPE TO EGISTO

Princeton, 22nd November

Dear Egisto,

Thank you for writing to me. Thank you for giving me frequent news of Alberico. I get news from Roberta when she phones me, but I get it in a much less summary form from your letters. He and I don't write to each other much.

I am glad you took him to Lucrezia's and that they have become friends. I like the idea of these two people I love being together and chatting. I like to think of them together, and I'm grateful to you for bringing them together.

There's one thing I find strange. You don't say whether you talked about me when you were at Lucrezia's that evening. You list the subjects of conversation, films, apartments, water-heaters and cutlets. But my name seems never to have been mentioned, as if I didn't exist, or were dead.

Though it's true that my flat in via Nazario Sauro was mentioned. I still think of it as mine, even though I've sold it. I don't know why but I don't consider the one I am living in in Princeton at the moment mine at all. It still seems to me to be my brother's and his wife's house. My brother is dead and his wife has married me. But then my first impression was that I was a stranger in the house and first impressions are sometimes ineradicable. And for this reason I continue to move about in this place like a stranger. I feel guilty if I happen to break a cup.

I am pleased you are reading my novel. Though I don't care about the novel at all now, and whenever it comes into my mind I experience a sensation of disgust. I wanted it to be published here and in Italy, but now I don't think I want it to be. Anyway a good three agencies have already turned it down.

I teach. I go cycling. I look after a child, Maggie, my wife's daughter's daughter. I look after her because her mother has gone away and Anne Marie is at her Institute all day, and anyway she doesn't like children.

Yours

Giuseppe

LUCREZIA TO GIUSEPPE

Rome, 26th November

A skinny girl, she wears spectacles. That's how you described Chantal in one of your letters years ago. You had just seen her for the first time. A skinny girl, she wears spectacles . A dress with four buttons down one side and four down the other. You mentioned her in passing, in the midst of various other things, and she didn't seem to have made such an impression on you. And then you go and fall in love with her. It happens. Well, yes, certainly I thought you might have when you told me how you went out together, and how you did the housework together. The life you described seemed to me to be cxtremely boring, but you told me about it in a very warm, excited way. Don't think I don't reread your letters. I often reread them.

In the room with the bear-cubs. Anne Marie with red blotches on her neck. The hamburger forgotten on your plate. Little Maggie. They made you sleep in the lumber-room. They've left you holding the baby. They use you as a baby-sitter. This is your life in America. My poor Giuseppe. You're in a really bad way.

Come back here. Pack your bags and come back here. Walk out on Anne Marie, Maggie, Danny and Mrs Mortimer. Come back here, where I am, your old faithful friend. I don't know what else to say.

Piero has a girl. He told me yesterday. She is called Diana and she is twenty-two. She is very beautiful, she has black hair and big eyes. I've seen a photograph of her. She is from Todi. She is a social worker. She's from a humble family, her father's a post-office employee. He met her last winter in Todi, during a concert. They were playing Ravel's *Bolero* when he and she exchanged a couple of words and a smile for the first time. She says she loves him, but she has a relationship with a student.

This torments Piero. On Saturdays she sees the student and because of this he almost always comes to Rome on Saturdays. He's not up to staying alone in Perugia, his mother Annina is there and at the moment he can't bear his mother's company. Also he thinks he ought to be with the children a bit. He goes for walks with the children and Joli. They go up to the Villa Borghese. The children are not really children any more, apart from little Vito, and they quickly get bored at the Villa Borghese and apart from Vito they go off and amuse themselves. They tell me they find Piero strange. They ask me what has happened to him. Sometimes he talks and talks and sometimes he smokes and smokes and doesn't say a syllable.

I didn't suspect anything. To tell you the truth I thought that over the past few months he wanted to suggest I go back to living with him again. He seemed to me to be acting like someone who wants to put back together again a marriage that has come apart. I had even prepared inside myself how I was going to refuse to do this – affectionately, calmly, firmly, very firmly and resolutely I was going to say to him that he must not on any account ever think of it again. Idiot, idiot. I didn't realise. Yesterday he told me everything. He has a girl. It is a serious matter, a serious commitment. He wants to marry her. He asked if I'd agree to divorce, but even so they'd have to wait five years and there was the risk she might go off with the other one in the meantime. She is a young, confused girl and she's not always sincere. I was dumbfounded. I had always believed myself to be the centre of his life, the centre of his thoughts. When I realized I wasn't, it was as if I had fallen from the top of a mountain. I was dumbfounded, and I was also, goodness knows why, suddenly very sad. I suddenly remembered all the saddest things in my life, my mother's illness, 'I' leaving me, the dead baby. I almost wept. Piero didn't notice. He doesn't see other people any more, he only sees that girl and himself. He went on talking, he kept me up till two in the morning.

This morning Zezé told me I looked ill. She asked if I was worried about money. She went to Piero who was in the kitchen making himself coffee. She told him I looked sick and was worried about money. Piero came and asked me if I was worried about money. I told him I have to buy a house and that houses cost money. I went out. I walked, despising myself, hating myself. I thought that I didn't have the right to shed a single tear about Piero's girl. What had happened to me wasn't unusual.

Piero went off again today. Alberico came to see me and stayed to supper. This will seem strange to you but Alberico often comes to my flat now. He is the one person in the world I feel good with.

I told him about Piero. I cried too. He didn't try to comfort me because there was nothing anyone could say.

Lucrezia

ALBINA TO GIUSEPPE

Luco dei Marsi, 3rd December

Dear Giuseppe,

You wrote to me when I got married and I never answered you. To tell the truth I haven't even written to you once since you've been in America.

Egisto came to see me here in Luco and we talked about you. I think your ears must have been burning. We talked about those lovely far-off times when we were all younger and we saw each other all the time. In fact those times are not so distant, but they seem very distant indeed, goodness knows why. And in fact we were not so young then, and we are not so old now.

I want to ask a favour of you. Perhaps you know that my husband and I have a little furniture factory here in Luco. We make reproduction antique furniture. Now we want to try our hand at making modern furniture too. I would be grateful if you could send me some American Interior Decorating Magazines. I can get ideas from them.

Some time ago I was in Rome to see Serena act in *Mirra*. We were all there, me, Egisto, Lucrezia, your cousin Roberta. Piero wasn't there.

I enjoyed myself. It was good.

I spent an afternoon with Lucrezia. I don't know what was wrong but it didn't go well, we both felt uncomfortable. Afterwards she told Egisto that I had become hard inside. Egisto passed this on to me. He was wrong to do this because there's never any need to tell someone the horrid things people say behind her back.

I haven't become hard. I talk about furniture a lot, and timber, and interior decorating. I talk about debts. My husband and I wake up at night to talk about debts, VAT, and all the other dreadful things. He gets up and makes himself hot, milky coffee.

Our business isn't going well. If things don't get better we shall be forced to close. Please send me the magazines.

How Lucrezia's children have changed. Cecilia wears stiletto heels. Vito has a key to the house and goes out to buy milk. And I found Graziano reading *Death in Venice*. Daniele and Augusto wouldn't even look me in the face. And we played so many games of football together on the lawn at *Le Margherite*. But they're not interested in me now because they're at an ungrateful age.

I often miss my bedsit, and my chats with Egisto, and our suppers at the Mariuccia Restaurant, which doesn't exist any more.

Albina

GIUSEPPE TO LUCREZIA

Princeton, 12th December

Dear Lucrezia,

Chantal came three days ago with a friend of hers and took the child. It was four in the afternoon. It was snowing. I hadn't taken the child to the nursery because she had a slight cold. She and I were in the sitting-room. She was sitting on the carpet playing with her dolls – she has lots of them. I was reading *Orlando Furioso*. I have to read it with my students and I have to be able to explain it.

Chantal arrived in a red Opel. I was standing at the window for a moment, watching the snow. She and her friend, a tall, thin girl with a long chin, got out of the car. I went out to them. Chantal had a red windcheater on, with a hood. She didn't even push her hood back. She told me she had come to collect the child and that she intended to leave at once. The Opel belonged to her friend. They had decided everything in a hurry and she hadn't had time to phone. In any case we knew that she would come sooner or later. She had left the commune and lived with her friend in a two-room apartment. She talked hurriedly and kept laughing in the shrill, dry, nervous way she has. The child was very happy to see her and wanted her to pick her up. I told her that the child had a cold but she said that didn't matter, they would wrap her up well, they had blankets in the car. I told her we ought to phone Anne Marie at the Institute, because she would come straight away. She said there wasn't time and in any case she didn't want to see her mother. She had a suitcase with her. She went into the room with the bear-cubs, took the child's clothes out of the drawers and stuffed them into the suitcase. There were still the toys, of which the child has an enormous number. Chantal told her friend to collect them together and to put them in the boot in a blanket. The friend went and fetched a blanket and made a bundle of the toys with it. Whilst they were getting in the car Mrs Mortimer appeared at the window of her house. She came out but Chantal had already got into the car with the child and just waved to her. The friend sat in the driver's seat. The Opel drove off and Mrs Mortimer and I were left standing in the road with the snow swirling around us.

Mrs Mortimer suggested I come into her house and have a cup of tea. I didn't want to at all but it seemed rude to refuse. Mrs Mortimer didn't make any comment about Chantal. She just said that it was a pity she had chosen such a cold day to travel on. Perhaps she saw me looking pale because she wanted to give me whisky instead of tea. Then she wanted to show me a cake she had made. It was in the oven and it wasn't ready yet, otherwise I could have tried it. She said that I would certainly miss the child because she was always with me. Sometimes she had heard me telling her little stories. They were really lovely and perhaps I could write them down and make them into a book. It might have better luck than my other book, which Anne Marie said had been turned down by no less than four agencies. I told her that it wasn't four but three. Anyway, she said, it had had bad luck. I finally managed to get back home. There were wardrobes standing open and empty in the room with the bear-cubs. However, I saw that Chantal had forgotten to take the child's vitamins, they were still on the chest of drawers. She had also forgotten them when she walked out of the house in Philadelphia.

Anne Marie came back at six as usual. I told her that Chantal had come and left again with Maggie. Anne Marie sat down in the hall, still in her coat; she took her cap off and patted her bun. She tried to keep her smile in place. She told me she didn't feel well and asked me to give her the tablets she takes when she feels dizzy. She said she wanted to lie down. I went upstairs with her and wanted to help her undress but she said she would do it by herself.

Chantal phoned the next day from New York. I answered the phone. She said they had arrived all right. An easy journey. I asked her if she wanted me to call her mother but she said no, it wasn't necessary, she had to leave for work. The child was staying with her friend, she would find a nursery for her later.

You see I have stopped being a baby-sitter. Chantal has given me the sack. I still sleep in what you call the lumber-room, though in fact it's an excellent room, even if there are piles of suitcases in it. I don't want to sleep in the room with the bear-cubs. It reminds me of both the child and of Chantal together.

Anne Marie and I are alone now, face to face, at meal times. These meal times are terrible. We each go about our own business for the rest of the time. Though last night she called me, I heard her from the ground floor and went up. She was ill. She wanted her tablets. She didn't have the strength to get up. I stayed with her for about an hour, until she slept. I held her hand and caressed her fingers. In the morning I made an appointment for her with a doctor. She will go next week.

I don't know what else to tell you today. I received the letter in which you told me about Piero. I can't offer you comfort because, as you put it, there is nothing anyone can say.

Giuseppe

ROBERTA TO GIUSEPPE

Rome, 20th December

Dear Giuseppe,

As I told you on the phone, Alberico is buying back your house from the Lanzaras. This seems an excellent idea, just that he's done everything in such a hurry, and if he had waited he might have got them to bring the price down. He said, and he kept on saying, that he thought it was too expensive. And then one morning he decided to buy it. Besides he doesn't have any money problems. And bricks and mortar don't let you down. There was a difficulty because Lanzara thought it improper to sell a house to an ex-patient of his. But then he thought about it and said that it didn't seem to him to be that serious an impropriety.

Yesterday Alberico and the Lanzaras went to a solicitor to draw up the agreement. The Lanzaras are leaving next month. They are moving to England. They have already started dismantling the bookcases.

As you can imagine, the idea of having Alberico on the floor above is one I like very much. I just hope that they don't make too much noise, because as you know Alberico is never alone. And now that Salvatore has come back to live with him again. Alberico didn't want him to because, Egisto told me, he thinks he is mixed up in some very shady business. What happened in piazza Tuscolo certainly makes you suspect it. It's never been clear why they attacked him, but it was probably something to do with a shady business deal. Alberico says he is not a weak person, he says he has a strong character, nevertheless he is weak in some things and he has been weak over Salvatore. He didn't want to, but he has welcomed him back. Salvatore was in a mental hospital for a while, then they discharged him and he went back to his mother's house in Frosinone, but he didn't want to stay in Frosinone and he found a job in Rome as a driver with a pharmaceutical firm. But he didn't have anywhere to sleep. He asked if he could have a bed at Alberico's place in piazza San Cosimato, at least for a few days, and then perhaps he'd come to some other arrangement. And so he came back and installed himself and his odds and ends in his old room. It doesn't matter, if they make a noise upstairs I shall put oropax in my ears. I've never used it but everyone says it's a great blessing.

Lucrezia has finally found a house too, and is in the process of buying it. It is a reasonably nice place, it's big, and Lucrezia is very pleased with it. The money she has isn't enough but Piero has told her she can borrow from a bank. The house is in via delle Medaglie d'Oro, not very far from here. Lucrezia found it by reading the advertisements in *Il Messaggero*. Alberico was at her house and they went to see it straightaway. Alberico and Lucrezia are now firm friends, they are always together. I imagine that this will please you. Two people you are fond of have met and become friends. Lucrezia hasn't called me to see the house, I haven't seen it yet. There was a time when Lucrezia was always 'phoning me and getting in touch with me, she used to say I was a comfort to her and reminded her of her mother a little. And then at a certain moment she stopped getting in touch, I don't know why. Clearly she has learnt to be an orphan.

Alberico's film *Deviance* has been very successful in France. He has another one nearly ready. He hasn't told me what it's called.

Ignazio Fegiz and Ippo, that friend of his, quarrelled and they were more or less about to separate, no one saw them for a while, and she wanted to sell her apartment and go and live in Fregene. It has a beautiful terrace and I was half thinking of buying it myself as an investment. He had fallen in love with a very beautiful eighteen-year-old girl. He wanted to marry her. But instead he stayed with Ippo. They are inseparable again. The Cat and the Fox. Now they've left for Vienna together. They will stay there for a fortnight seeing the galleries and museums. Egisto told me, he always knows everyone's business. It seems that she isn't going to sell her apartment any more.

Lucrezia is going to Paris with Serena, Vito and Cecilia, for the New Year. The other children are going to Perugia. But really they aren't children any more.

Give me news of Anne Marie's health. You seemed a little worried about her on the phone.

With love from

Roberta

LUCREZIA TO GIUSEPPE

Rome, 22nd December

I went to Monte Fermo with Alberico, Vito, Cecilia and Joli. I asked Alberico to come along with us. I couldn't have gone alone with Cecilia and Vito, it would have upset me. But I became very upset anyway when we came back.

We didn't go in my Volkswagen, we went in Alberico's car. He has a new car, a pale blue Prisma. It's being run in. He enjoys running it in.

It was a beautiful sunny day. We got out for a moment at Monte Fermo to have a coffee. They recognized me and made a fuss of me. There was the man who used to sell mushrooms, and the old woman with her basket of eggs. Monte Fermo is just the same, nothing has changed.

Then we went to *Le Margherite*. To what was *Le Margherite*. Now they've made a hotel out of it. It's called the Hotel Panorama.

It is impossible to recognize our house in the Hotel Panorama. It was yellow and old with stone balconies. The Hotel Panorama looks new. It is half cherry-pink and half sky-blue. There are geraniums on the balconies. The balconies are long and narrow, with an iron railing. The old porch has gone. They have put white metal tables out at the front, and deckchairs and swings, under a fringed canvas awning. At the back where the little hazel tree used to be there is a swimming pool with clear, clean water in it, with more deckchairs around the edge. Inside you can see floors with white and brown patterns on them, corridors and rooms. There was a chamber-maid with a bucket and a floor cloth. There didn't seem to be a single guest. We left.

We bought bread and ham in Monte Fermo. They told us that the Hotel Panorama was doing badly and is on the point of bankruptcy. It's open the whole year, but lord knows who for. They might make it into a college for land-surveying. No one knows yet.

We stopped in Pianura too. Where the Women's Centre used to be there is an electrical repair shop for cars.

I am buying a house. I don't enjoy living in Rome but then I don't know where I'd enjoy living. The flat I might buy is in viale Medaglie d'Oro. I hate that area, but the flat isn't too bad. It's on the top floor, and has a balcony. I'm getting a loan from a bank.

Piero phones me every morning from Perugia nowadays. He used to be against long-distance telephone calls but now he keeps me on the 'phone for ages. I want to talk to him about houses, money, and the loan, but he does nothing but talk about himself and about this girl Diana, what she said to him and what she didn't say to him. He's just the same when he comes to Rome. He says he comes for the children's sake, but then instead of being with the children he talks to me. He hasn't anyone else to talk to, only me. I listen to him, what else can I do? He seems to me to be floundering about in very deep water.

Alberico is buying what used to be your flat. Seen from the outside the house is still the same, and the street is still the same too. Though the Mariuccia Restaurant isn't there any more, nor the Cafe Esperia. Where the Cafe Esperia used to be there's a shop called *La Casa del Tortellino*. There isn't anything where the Mariuccia Restaurant used to be. There's a grating. Behind the grating there are some sacks of cement. People say there's going to be a laundry there.

Alberico often eats at our house. Perhaps because of this I've started to quite enjoy cooking again. Because he eats here so often. I think about which dishes to prepare and talk it over with Zezé. I don't cook meat loaf, because my meat loaves fall apart, and it's always a mistake when a meat loaf falls apart, even if it's good.

I'm leaving in a few days, I'm going to Paris with Serena for a fortnight. Serena has borrowed a little flat. I shall leave the children in Rome with Zezé who has agreed to stay and sleep here.

I've never been to Paris in my life and Serena says this is ridiculous. I've never been on any long journeys. And I've never really been on holiday. There was almost always cooking to do and beds to make, even on holiday. But I don't want to complain. I know I'm better off than most.

Roberta said your wife is ill. Write and tell me what's the matter with her. Send me your news. I hope that you have stopped thinking about Chantal.

I wish you a happy Christmas

Lucrezia

ALBERICO TO GIUSEPPE

Rome, 27th December

My dear father,

I was very pleased to get your 'phone call on Christmas Day. Thank you. You must have heard a great deal of noise. There were a lot of us. The lady who comes in the mornings had cooked us a roast turkey. She won't come for a while now because Lucrezia is going away and leaving her children in Rome; she will go to Lucrezia's house for the whole day. Salvatore and I washed up the plates from the Christmas lunch. There were piles of them.

Yes, I am buying your famous house in via Nazario Sauro. Famous because after you sold it you started to regret having done so, and to complain to me and to other people about how you had been a real imbecile to sell it. Well, now it's yours again. Or rather it's mine, but if you come back to Italy and you want to live there you can. I would gladly let you have it.

Meanwhile I shall move in very shortly, as soon as the Lanzaras leave. If you come to Rome soon, as you say you will, you could be my guest in via Nazario Sauro. We could live together for a short time, not for too long because you wouldn't enjoy it and neither would I. I said you could be my guest, but as you are my father you wouldn't be a guest. I remember that you always used to say you didn't like being a guest, and you liked having guests even less. I don't remember many of the things you used to say, just a few. To tell you the honest truth I can only remember you very slightly and very vaguely.

I know that your wife isn't well. I'm sorry. I know that the little girl isn't with you any more. Her mother came and collected her. Lucrezia told me. I'm sorry about that too. Though it is right that the child should be with her mother, as she has a mother.

With love and best wishes from Alberico

GIUSEPPE TO ALBERICO

Princeton, 7th January

My dearest son,

Anne Marie is very ill. They have discovered that she has leukemia very seriously, and there's no hope. The doctors have told me that she will not live long. Every day I go with her to a clinic where they give her blood transfusions. We go and come back in a taxi because as you know I can't drive, and Anne Marie no longer has the strength to drive. She has no strength whatsoever. It is very tiring for her to get out of bed and to move about. In the space of a few days she has got much worse, a few weeks ago she didn't feel well but she still drove her car and went to the Institute. Now I can never leave her. When I go to give my lessons I call our neighbour Mrs Mortimer over.

Chantal, Anne Marie's daughter, is in New York and doesn't come very often. She can't because she would lose her job. She is a waitress in a restaurant. And she has the child too. Since she has known that her mother is ill she has come three times. She didn't bring the child with her. She says that the child is doing very well, that she is thriving much better than when she was with us. This hurt me, but Chantal is someone who can sometimes say cruel things without realizing it. She also told me that the child never mentions me. She stayed for a short time then left quickly. Apart from me and Mrs Mortimer, Anne Marie doesn't have anyone.

I think that Anne Marie has realized she is dying. I think she thinks about it all the time, but she never says what she is thinking. She is a woman who never says what she is thinking. I've become aware that in the two years we have been married, I have never once felt that she was telling me what she really thought.

Thank you for your letter, and thank you for buying back my

famous house. I can't help but think you are buying it back because it was mine. I haven't had another house after that one. The house where I live now is profoundly alien to me, and it always has been. Perhaps because I've never thought of living in America for good.

I'm extremely pleased that you see Lucrezia so often. I thank you for that too, that you are such good friends with Lucrezia, and that you so often spend time with her. I could certainly have introduced you to each other when I was in Italy. I've no idea why I didn't. That you have become friends now is like receiving an unexpected gift. I often think of you both in a room I don't know but can imagine, because it probably has the furniture I used to see at *Le Margherite*, and which I remember so well. I know that you and Lucrezia went to *Le Margherite*. She wrote and told me. I know that you have a pale blue Prisma.

With love from

your father

PIERO TO GIUSEPPE

Perugia, 13th January

My dearest Giuseppe,

I am here, close to you, with my old loyal affection for you.

I didn't come to Rome that day because I had an engagement in Perugia I couldn't possibly put off. And even Lucrezia wasn't in Rome, she was in Paris where she still is. I telephoned Serena who is there with her, and asked her not to let her see the Italian newspapers, and to say nothing. You know that recently Alberico and Lucrezia had become great friends. They were always together. And so I want to be the one who tells her, tomorrow, when she gets back. Serena has told her that Alberico doesn't answer the telephone because he has gone to Vienna for a holiday and that we don't know his address.

I know that you only stayed in Rome for three days because your wife is very ill and you had to go back to her immediately.

I haven't written to you for a long time but I've had news of you from Lucrezia. It was good news too, but now your wife is seriously ill, and suddenly this new terrible disaster has happened to you.

With love from

Piero

EGISTO TO IGNAZIO FEGIZ

Rome, 15th January

Dear Ignazio,

I got your address in Vienna from Ippo's concierge. I don't know if you have read the Italian newspapers. I suppose you probably haven't read them. Alberico is dead. He was killed in an alley off Trastevere, behind his house, on the 7th January.

He was typing, alone in his house. It was eleven at night. Salvatore, Adelmo and Gianni had gone down to have a cappuccino. Gianni came up and told him that Salvatore had picked a fight in an alley near piazza San Callisto. Alberico and Gianni went down. They met Adelmo in the street, and he tried to hold them back. They didn't take any notice of him and Adelmo followed them. What we know, we know from Adelmo and Gianni. There was a group of people fighting in the alley. They caught sight of Salvatore's red jumper. Alberico ran over to him and tried to drag him away. There were some people standing watching but none of them made a move. Adelmo thinks that among them he recognized the two on the scooter whom he had seen in piazza Tuscolo, and also another one with a blond ponytail who had been in piazza Tuscolo. Then Adelmo saw that Salvatore had a knife. Someone snatched it from him. Alberico fell and got up again. They stabbed him as he was getting up. Salvatore screamed and they threw themselves on top of him. Salvatore died immediately. Alberico died after half an hour. Someone called the emergency services, then an ambulance came, and then the police jeeps.

I had just got back from the newspaper when Gianni called me. Gianni and Adelmo were at the Santo Spirito hospital. Alberico died without regaining consciousness.

The same thing happened to Nadia. The same fate.

Adelmo and I went to his flat to collect his clothes. We phoned Roberta but we didn't know how to tell the poor woman what had happened. She was very fond of Alberico, they were cousins. Adelmo went to her house to tell her.

We phoned Giuseppe in America. He came. He was here for the funeral. But he left immediately because his wife is gravely ill, and there wasn't anyone with her.

Lucrezia was in Paris. They didn't tell her anything. They kept the newspapers hidden. Piero told her when she came back. The funeral was already over, Giuseppe had already left. And so Giuseppe and Lucrezia didn't see each other again.

I think it's very bad that they didn't tell Lucrezia. She and Alberico were friends, over the last few months they were always together. But Piero wanted it like this.

In the district where Alberico lived they are in mourning for him. They remember him as courteous and gentle when he went into the shops and stopped to chat with this person or that person. He was generous, he lent money to whoever needed it, and in a way he gave it to them because he never asked for it back again. They also mourn for Salvatore, and they remember him too. Gentle he wasn't, he had quarrelled with everyone in the district, he was quick with his fists. But they had known him for a while and it shocks them to think of him as dead now. Some say that Salvatore was a police informer. Others say he pushed drugs. Others say he lent money at a high rate of interest. Others say he sent anonymous letters. Everyone thinks that the same people were involved in piazza Tuscolo and in vicolo Sant' Apollinare, and Adelmo insists that in both places there was a man with a blond pony-tail. But people say that after what happened in piazza Tuscolo whoever it was would have cut it off so as not to be recognized. The police think that Adelmo has imagined the blond pony-tail, both this time and the previous time.

Giuseppe and Salvatore's mother will have to initiate civil proceedings against persons unknown.

Remember me to Ippo,

Egisto

EGISTO TO ALBINA

Rome, 2nd February

Dear Albina,

I saw you on the day of the funeral, but then I immediately lost you and I looked for you without finding you again. Adelmo told me that you had gone straight back to Luco dei Marsi.

With Adelmo and Gianni I put Alberico's papers in order, in the flat below me. We put all the papers, the ideas for films and the screen plays into a trunk, which we loaded on to my car and took to Roberta's house in via Nazario Sauro. Alberico didn't have many books. His clothes were just a few odds and ends and the cleaning woman, Zezé, took these away. She gave them to some old people who live near her. The furniture consisted of a table and two or three wardrobes that were falling to pieces, bought in Porta Portese. Zezé took them away too.

We spent two or three afternoons emptying the flat. Then we returned the keys to the landlady.

The idea of having that flat empty underneath me really upsets me. I want to get out of this house. I have too many memories here. But as you know it's not easy to find somewhere to rent in Rome. You can find a place to buy but I don't have enough money.

Alberico had not bought the house in via Nazario Sauro, the one that is above Roberta and that used to belong to Giuseppe, he had only signed the agreement. The Lanzaras have given the advance back to Roberta, who is taking care of these practical things. Everything that Alberico possessed will go to Nadia's daughter, Giorgina, the child he had registered as his. Giorgina lives in Sicily with her maternal grandparents who are millionaires, and she is a millionaire too. It's a pity that all that money Alberico had should go to someone who doesn't need it, when there are so many people living in want. It's true that it's no one's fault, but it makes you feel bad.

I saw Giuseppe at the funeral and I spent a few hours with him afterwards. I thought he had aged a great deal. According to Adelmo, he has the eyes of someone who drinks spirits far too much. But that might just be a fantasy of Adelmo's. Poor Giuseppe, he was in a wretched state, the news had reached him in America whilst he was looking after his wife who is dying. I don't know if she is dead now or not. He went straight back.

I spent a lot of time with Alberico, I was very attached to him. I miss him. I try and be alone as little as possible. I go to the newspaper, I wander about, I go and see Serena act. Anything not to be alone. Sometimes I pass that damned alley. It is strange how places that make us sad attract us. They attract and repel us. Just as I want to get out of this house, but at the same time I want to stay here for ever.

With love from

Egisto

GIUSEPPE TO LUCREZIA

Princeton, 20th February

My Lucrezia,

That day you phoned me we hardly said anything to each other. I cried. And you cried too. It was a long-distance weep.

You asked me if I were coming back to Italy. I didn't know how to answer you. I was not up to making plans. I'm not up to it now either. My head is in a whirl.

Anne Marie died on the 16th February, four days ago. She died in hospital. Chantal and I were there.

I 'phoned Danny to tell him. He came. He was there at the funeral too. He and Chantal are icy cold with each other. He came for my sake. Chantal left immediately after the funeral. Danny stayed with me, until yesterday.

Danny is the only friend I have here. We get on well together, despite the difference in age. He could be my son. Alberico was about his age, twenty-six.

Chantal told me that I get on well with Danny because he is like me, someone outside of reality. I don't know if I am outside of reality, and I don't know if Danny is. Above all I don't know what reality is for Chantal.

Danny is out of work again. He had found employment in a circulating library, he was completely happy, and after a month they fired him. He had forgotten to catalogue some books. I think he's very disorganized and absent-minded in his work.

Chantal is disorganized and absent-minded too, but not in her work. In her work I think she is punctilious and precise.

When we see each other Danny usually asks me to lend him money. And then he might well pay it back, but the next time he asks again. If anyone else asked me it would annoy me. But it doesn't cost me anything to give him money, and in a way I like to.

If Alberico had not been my son I might have been able to get on well with him, as I get on well with Danny. The fact that we were father and son spoilt everything. It made us embarrssed, stupid, cold, and often insincere. However, I never tried to improve our relationship. It always seemed to me that there was plenty of time. And now this makes me very unhappy.

I talked to Danny for a long time about Alberico. We stayed up till two in the morning.

We also talked about Chantal, about Anne Marie, about the child. We talked about the dead and the living. Finally I told him that I had been in love with Chantal. As I was saying this, I felt I was recounting a story that had happened a very long time ago, years and years ago.

During those days in Rome I didn't see anyone except Egisto and Roberta. I stayed in a hotel in piazza della Minerva. I didn't go to via Nazario Sauro.

If I return to Italy I shall have to look for a house. As you have perhaps heard, Alberico had not yet bought the house in via Nazario Sauro.

Perhaps the words 'If I return' sound strange to you. Perhaps the conditional sounds strange to you. But at the moment everything seems uncertain to me, and I don't know how to find my way through the tangle of my thoughts. I want to return to Italy, and at the same time I don't want to return at all. I long to see you, Lucrezia, and at the same time I don't want to see you at all. I am afraid of seeing you, of finding myself face to face with you. We have been apart for too long, and too many things have happened, to you and to me.

Giuseppe

LUCREZIA TO GIUSEPPE

Rome, 5th March

I am sorry that your wife has died.

I am very, very sorry that we did not meet when you came to Rome.

I don't know how to forgive Piero for telling Serena to keep the newspapers hidden from me. And so I didn't know anything. Those days were quite happy days for me. I wandered around Paris with Serena, we bought stockings, ate in restaurants, looked at pictures.

Serena knew and said nothing to me. Piero had 'phoned her on the morning of 8th January. She seemed a little strange to me for a few moments, she said she had a headache.

When I got back to Rome, Piero told me.

I'm glad that I went to Monte Fermo that time, in the pale blue Prisma. I'm glad that we saw the Hotel Panorama.

Alberico wasn't happy, but he often laughed. I laughed with him. It was marvellous to laugh together

When he laughed you could see his little white teeth.

I would have fallen in love with him, if he hadn't been a homosexual. As he was, no – because I could never fall in love with a homosexual. We were friends, it was the kind of friendship that stays on one level and never changes, it remains secure and the same for ever.

You and I are friends too. But we haven't always been friends, before we were friends we were lovers. And we have also had a son together, Graziano. You have always pretended that it wasn't true.

And now you have been away for a long time and I no longer know what you are like, and you no longer know what I am like.

You say that you long to see me again, and at the same time

you don't want to see me at all. I understand you. It's the same for me.

I said before that I was sorry your wife had died. It isn't true, I'm not sorry at all. In the first place I didn't know her, and in the second place I know very well that you were not happy with her, and that you married her for no apparent reason.

One day, about a week ago, 'I' phoned me. He asked if he could come and see me because he wanted to talk to me. He came with Ippo. It seemed so strange to me, to see them both in front of me. The Cat and the Fox. I served them tea.

Ippo is a little old woman. I saw her close up, she is a little old woman. I looked at her curiously, without hatred. It is difficult to hate little old women. You talk loudly to them, because they might be a bit deaf.

'I' sat in the armchair he always sat in when he used to come and see me every day, when we were lovers. I looked at his large, florid face, his grey crew-cut. I asked myself however could I have suffered so much for that face, for that body in its overcoat. He didn't even take off his overcoat. It's true that before, when we were lovers, he was always complaining about how cold my house was.

A face, a body, an overcoat – nothing mysterious about them, without any secrets, harmless.

We also had a son together. It wasn't very long ago.

Guess what they wanted. They wanted to ask me if I knew anything about the house in via Nazario Sauro. Ippo would like to buy it. Because her own is so very small and besides she has money to invest. The Lanzaras have left, and she didn't know who to turn to. She thought of Roberta who lives there, on the floor below. She doesn't know her personally. 'I' knows her well. But he hasn't seen her for so long, and he dare not phone her. They wanted me to be a go-between. I called Roberta on the phone straight away and told her that 'I' wanted to talk to her. She was very surprised. 'I' talked to her and they arranged to meet. Roberta has the keys. The Lanzaras left them with her. I think Ippo and 'I' will buy that house and go and live there together.

You used to say about 'I' that he always kept one hand behind his back. It's true. I saw that closed fist behind his back as he was walking towards the door. You used to say 'Goodness only knows what's in that hand'. There is nothing in that hand. Nothing.

It's true that during these past few years too many things have happened, to you and to me. Because of this, if we were to see each other again, we wouldn't be able to speak for a while.

I've used the conditional too, goodness knows why. Why ever shouldn't we see each other again, in this life or the next?

It isn't true that I no longer know what you are like. I know very well what you are like. I remember you as if I had you here in front of me.

Your long thinning hair. Your glasses. Your long nose. Your long, bony legs. Your big hands. They were always cold, even when the weather was hot. That's how I remember you.

Lucrezia